THIS DISTANCE

a collection of short stories by Nick Gregorio

maudlinhouse.net
twitter.com/maudlinhouse

ISBN 13: 978-0-9994723-2-3
ISBN-10: 0-9994723-2-1

This Distance
Copyright © 2018 by Nick Gregorio

All rights reserved. No part of this book may be reproduced in any form by any electronic or mechanical means including photocopying, recording, or information storage and retrieval without permission in writing from the author.

For Lizz, who closed the distance for me.

"Maybe you've had skin next to your skin, but when was the last time you let yourself be touched?"

—Tom Spanbauer, *In the City of Shy Hunters*

"Thought it over, thought I'd walk over,
And over coffee we could chat,
But then, then I thought again.
'Cause what was was over and now I know that.
Thought I'd call, we could talk it over.
I knew that wouldn't work somehow.
What was was over and I should just get over,
And that is where I'm at right now."

—The Mighty Mighty BossToneS, "What Was Was Over"

"Take luck! Take luck and care. Take care of the luck! Good luck taking care of the, the luck that you might have, if you have luck, take it, and care for it. Take luck care of it...You're sure to see them again."

—Brian Regan

Contents

A Lesson in Theoretical Physics 1
Goings-On & Happenstance 5
I Sing the Body Electric Blue 17
This Distance 21
Yeah? Well My Friend Chris Hemsworth
   Says You Ain't Shit 25
It's Always Something, It's Never Nothing 29
Embracing Skeletons 41
Drag 55
Life/Hack 57
LIV 71
Beginning Again, Or How to Murder Your Monster and
   Get Away with It 83
Hero Complex 91
Muncy 105
Stars & Star Maps 113
Love & Marriage & Love & Marriage 115
The Beyond 121
Me and You on Regis-132 129
Lost in Space 133
Darwin 145
Death Protects 147
Coffee Mug 151
He's Doing Just Fine 153
The Slipper People 167
Wake Up Dead 173
Acknowledgments 177
About the Author 181

A Lesson in Theoretical Physics

Forget mathematical equations or people in white coats wearing glasses that double, triple the size of their eyes. Forget words like Quantum Field Theory. Don't go into bookstores asking to be pointed to the science section.

Just don't. Forget it.

We, all of us, vibrate at a frequency that allows us to perceive one another in a three-dimensional space. We can talk to one another, touch one another, see, smell, taste one another. We can move forward, backward, left, right, up, down, all around. Examine everything from every angle. Every wrinkle, fold, and follicle.

It's all there. The potential to understand each other.

Even after someone's gone.

Think about it this way: Say you're trying to show a sphere to a two-dimensional stickman. You smush a ball into his flat world and ask him to describe what he saw. He'd tell you all he saw was a dot that turned into a small circle, then a bigger circle, and then shrunk back down to a dot again before disappearing. Your stickman will never be able to comprehend the sphere. It will never be a ball to him. Just an unexplainable phenomenon.

We're stick-people when we try to perceive fourth, fifth, sixth-dimensional stuff, beings—whatever.

But the part that's so fantastical is that, according to theoretical physicists, we may occupy the same space as extra-dimensional somethings. We just vibrate on a frequency that doesn't allow us to understand them.

But they're there.

All the time.

They're sitting in the chair you're in right now. Sleeping in your bed. Using your toilet. Reading your books, watching your DVDs, rifling through your internet search history. To them, your stuff is their stuff. You may not even exist to them, same way they don't to us. But they're there.

It's different, of course, when someone leaves.

They don't exit our plane of existence, they're just gone.

But you could drive past them every morning on your way to work.

Walk the same steps they took on their way across the gym parking lot—the atoms from the soles of their running sneakers clinging to yours.

Run your fingers along the same cans of soup at the supermarket they may have just touched—the kind you know they eat after a horrible day at the office.

Sit in a movie theater seat they may have just left their butt-print in—the same butt-print that used to be on your couch, your bed, haloed in steam on the glass shower wall.

There's comfort in that like there's wonder in extra-dimensional whatevers.

No, they're not in and around you like the things out in the multiverse.

But there's always a chance of breathing in a wisp of the carbon dioxide they let go of just now.

Now.

And now.

There's always the possibility that a molecule of skin'll get left behind on a door handle at the mall, or the drugstore, or the restaurant you went to together all the time.

There's always the hope that the hair clinging to your pea coat could be theirs. That the smudge on your pint glass is from their lips.

All of the theories and conjecture are better than nothingness.

Traditional science says that more than likely we're alone in our universe. So far from anything else—if there is anything else—that we're impossible to find.

But, just for a minute, accept the idea that an empty room could be full.

Doesn't matter with what.

Because then even the blackest, darkest spaces are stuffed with infinity.

Because then an endless multiverse doesn't have to be a lonely place.

It can be full.

Of smells, tastes, sounds. Of spectral near-misses. Of the possibility of anything, everything.

When anything is possible nothing's not.

Math, scientists, tongue-twisty theories, a bunch of books—they're all fine. They'll give you reasons. Provide proof.

But really, what proof do you need? You're breathing the same air. Walking the same sidewalks. Feeling the same sun.

You can't see them.

But they're there.

Goings-On & Happenstance

She found him in bed with another woman on a Tuesday.

That Wednesday, when she was describing what she'd seen, she replaced "in" with "on." It was more accurate. It painted a better picture.

They hadn't even taken the throw pillows off the bed.

"They must've planned it that way," she said. Jim would have been able to smooth away two sets of knee prints, a pair of hands. But she'd caught him.

And she'd watched for a minute. Not because she was turned on, that would've been ridiculous. Before then she'd never seen what his ass looked like in that set of circumstances.

When she obsessed about the incident that Thursday night she couldn't remember if she'd ever noticed how pock-marked those flat cheeks of his were. Craggy and white, it reminded her of when she was a teenager, of what her own bare ass must have looked like pressed against the passenger window as she and her friends drove past movie theater marquees.

She said, "Never thought of it that way," sitting at the dinner table, staring at the food she hadn't touched, at the phone that was spinning on its own axis as it vibrated from the calls she wasn't picking up. The sound it made on the table reminded her of the garage door opening, of his coming home from work. But the front door never opened. And she sat there until she went and curled herself up on the couch.

In the morning, Friday, she counted Jim's missed calls. She waited until lunch to listen to his voicemails. They were composed at first, almost professional.

"Hi. It's me. Listen, I think we should get together. Talk about what happened the other night."

And then less so.

"Come on. Call me back. Please? You know me, okay? You know I love you. You know that. This has nothing to do with what I feel for you. You're my best friend."

And then, "Please fucking call me back. Please? I'm sick. I think I'm sick. I must be, right? Who does shit like this? Sick people. I'm sick."

She sat with her legs crossed on a park bench smoking a Camel, her thumb hovering over the phone, over the send key. She couldn't remember the last time she'd smoked. Before the wedding. Jim had asked her to quit, said, "I want us to have a long life together."

She called her husband. But ended the call before the first ring.

And then she had to redo her makeup before heading back to the office.

On Saturday she was pulling into the parking lot of the neutral establishment they'd agreed upon while she was halfway through a bottle of wine late the night before. She checked her makeup in the mirror, pulled open the car door, counted her steps on the macadam.

Then she remembered having his hand down her pants in that lot. Years ago. In his old car, listening to Sara Bareilles' "Love Song" on the radio.

She turned back to her car but stopped when she heard him call her name from underneath the diner's signage.

Once inside and in a booth, Jim ordered a coffee, said, "Black."

"It comes black," she said, pointing to a bowl of creamers at the end of the table.

She continued to put him down in small ways. It wasn't what she'd planned on doing. She'd shown up with a plan. With questions to ask. But instead, she told him they were going to spit on his burger because he asked for the bacon extra crispy. She said they're rubbing the napkins he asked for under their armpits. She told him he should have gotten his mother to iron his shirt, it looks like it came out of the hamper. She said, "That is where you're staying right now, right? Your mother's?"

"Stop," he said.

But he still lifted the bun, checked for a loogie. He sniffed the napkins before wiping his mouth. He patted his shirt down as if his skin could steam the fabric flat.

She ate nothing, let her coffee get cold, tried to think of ways to—at the very least—be cordial.

They were there an hour. He must have said how sorry he was a dozen times, promised it would never happen again a dozen more, but she lost count of both once he began getting choked up.

She said, "Don't. Don't do that. You don't get to do that."

"I don't know what else to say."

"How about you tell me what I'm supposed to do? Can you do that? What do I do now?"

Jim didn't say anything. He balled up a napkin, sipped his coffee, stared at the table. But said nothing.

So she left.

She came inches from backing over him in the parking lot after he followed her to her car, calling her name, saying please, asking for her not to leave.

By the time she reached the stoplight she was asking herself the questions she'd prepared for him. When she turned onto the main road her words were more a series of screams than anything else. Then she pulled over and waited for her breathing to level out.

• • •

On Match.com, she used the name Meredith.

On OkCupid, she called herself Ellie.

On Plenty of Fish, Laurel.

After several months of ending some of Jim's calls midsentence, ignoring others, changing locks, dropping clothes in unmarked cardboard boxes on his mother's porch, she took the advice from some friends at work.

They'd told her to go have some fun. Go meet people.

"Get yourself laid," they'd said.

It took a few attempts from her friends to convince her it wasn't revenge. They'd said revenge is petty.

"Think of it as justice."

A muscle relaxer and a glass of wine while watching *Grey's Anatomy* allowed her to open her laptop. She faked the names because it was sort of fun. She picked them from the list she and her husband compiled for their future daughters if ever they were to have any. While she was showering the next morning, she regretted using them. She had to sit down in the tub, let hot water rain on her as some form of punishment for giving away the names of little girls with golden hair who knew nothing of adult goings-on.

She spent most of the morning at work clearing her inbox of notifications from the dating sites.

Pootieboi sent you a message.

DanielB winked at you.

BSGFan75 liked your photo.

During her smoke break in the park, her friend asked her what she was so afraid of, told her it's not a big deal.

She said, "If I go and do this, it'll mean it's really over. My marriage. The life I've been living."

Her friend said, "Honey. It already is over."

She said she didn't even use her real name.

"So? Maybe it won't hurt to pretend to be someone else for a while."

She made dinner that night, a meal she would prepare on special occasions. Date nights. And she ate it alone, the television holding conversations in the living room.

She had seconds. Did the dishes. Talked herself through the responses she would write once she loaded the dishwasher. And then once she put a load of laundry in the machine. And then after she cleaned the bathroom.

Then she figured she may as well sleep on it.

But she didn't sleep. Nick at Nite played the same episode of *The New Adventures of Old Christine* she'd seen the week before. And the ceiling began to bore her.

So she wrote responses from Meredith in which she was enthusiastic and funny. A bit snarky. But in a good-natured way.

Ellie was more reserved, more calculated with her choice of words. Her dry wit would be something the guys she wrote to would want to tell their friends about.

Laurel liked to party. But she wasn't some sort of slut. She liked to go out on weekends and dance, and she made it clear that the type of guy she wanted to meet should be one who has some moves. If not, sorry, he just wasn't her type.

In the morning she realized she hadn't removed her makeup. A Rorschach test was left on her pillowcase in Almay.

• • •

Meredith met David at a microbrewery outside the city. She watched him watch her park her car, standing under the terrace leading into the old converted inn. They smiled, hugged, bent at the hip so only their shoulders touched.

David asked for menus after picking a place at the corner of the bar, said, "This place has incredible food."

They finished their first round of beers before they ordered anything to eat. They had their second before the plates were clunked onto the bar.

When Meredith finished her fourth saison she forgot about her distaste for beer, forgot to be conscious of how she was eating.

David pointed to his lip.

Meredith, mouth full, said, "Hmm?"

He smiled, reached over the corner of the bar, and wiped her bottom lip. His thumb came away with a glob of chipotle aioli.

She considered licking the sauce from his thumb, make a show of it. But David wiped it on his napkin, and "slut" bounced around Meredith's skull until the bartender placed another beer in front of her.

David insisted on paying, he said, "Please. Think of it as a thank you for spending the night with me."

Meredith said, "But we haven't spent the night together yet."

She made faces at herself over how stupid that must have sounded as David put his hand on the small of her back, ushered her out into the parking lot.

They were awkward standing next to Meredith's car until David leaned in and kissed her.

Meredith shoved her body into his, wrapped her arms around his neck. She was aware of the sounds their mouths were making. Their lips smacking together, the sucking noises. She wondered if her tongue was too aggressive, if maybe he was thinking she was taking over the situation, emasculating him.

She pulled away.

David asked her, "What now?"

Meredith told him to follow her home.

In the car, on the phone with her friend from work, she said she was crazy. "This is crazy, right?"

Her friend said no, told her to stop over-thinking this. "It's just sex," her friend said.

"Is it, though?"

"Of course it is."

Meredith ended the call when she pulled into her driveway. She waited for David to get to the porch, took his hand.

As they walked through the living room, past the kitchen, David kept saying things about how he hopes she doesn't think he was expecting this. "This isn't something I do," he said.

In the bedroom, Meredith unbuckled his belt, told him not to worry. She said, "I want this."

Once their clothes were all over the bedroom she bent over in front of him. After a while, after she said, "Harder," and, "Harder than that," she told him to smack her ass.

And he did.

Meredith yelped.

David asked her if she was okay, if he hurt her.

"Yeah, that was good," she said. "Do it again."

She was on top of David for the rest of it. She kept her eyes closed, raked her nails over his chest, felt torn skin roll up underneath her acrylics. She never once looked to see what his face was morphing into as he grunted.

The headboard was ramming into the wall toward the end. And Meredith took note of how fast the collisions were coming. She took David's hand, wrapped it around her throat, and counted specs of light on her eyelids.

Then she said, "Hit me."

"What?"

"Hit me."

David slapped her across the face. It didn't make much of a noise, didn't feel the way Meredith hoped. She said, "Again. Harder this time."

The next slap echoed off the walls, threw Meredith's face to the side, split her lip at the corner. And she rode him harder.

When she stopped grinding herself into him, she took in several short breaths, and climbed off.

She didn't fall into bed next to him. She didn't cover herself as she walked across the room. She closed and locked the bathroom door, and laid the tile floor, curling her knees up to her chest.

David knocked, asked if she was okay, apologized for doing something wrong, if he'd done something wrong.

"I feel sick," she said. "I think I drank too much. I'm sorry."

David asked if he should stay.

"No, it's okay. You don't have to."

She waited until she heard David leave. And when he was gone she called her husband.

• • •

She lied to her friends at work on Monday about how her date had gone, told them nothing happened. "I made a pot of coffee and we talked until he went home."

"Are you planning on seeing him again?"

"I don't see why not."

"Did you do anything else over the weekend?"

She didn't tell them that she'd gone around the house re-hanging all the photos of her and Jim she'd taken down. Or that she'd cleared out the drawers in the bureaus she'd filled with her clothes so there would be room for his things. Or that she and Jim had had sex a handful of times, and she'd done things she used to tell him she wouldn't do to prove to herself she wasn't as awful as she felt.

She said, "Nope. Watched a movie. Ordered pizza."

On Tuesday she gave up smoking again. That morning Jim asked her why her clothes smelled. And she told him. She said, "I've been smoking."

He asked her if it was because of him, because of what he'd done.

"It was a reaction," she said. "It helped."

Standing in a towel, fresh from the shower, he sat on the bed, and told her that he loved her. That nothing like that will ever happen again. He said things that she'd read in bad romance novels about cheating husbands. She could have sworn something he'd said came out of a romcom. And she let him go on and on, recite lines about love and loss and infidelity. She stood, arms crossed, reveling in it for a moment.

Until she thought of David—who'd been texting her since Friday night—and broke all of her cigarettes in half before she left for work.

At lunch, her friend came to her cube, said, "Ready?"

"I think I'll eat lunch here. Lots of work to do."

"Smoke break?"

"Too busy. But thanks."

She ignored texts from David for the rest of the day.

"Hey," his first text read. "Listen, things got a little nuts the other night. I think we need to talk about it. Please give me a call when you can."

By late afternoon they became a bit more panicked.

"Meredith, I'm not the kind of guy who does that sort of thing. Please call me. I feel like I really crossed a line. Just let me know you're okay."

She shut her phone off when she got home, after David's

final text.

"Meredith? You're scaring me. I just want to know if you're okay. I'm fucking freaking out here. I'll be available to talk after seven. Call me."

By seven she and Jim were in the bathtub together. A half-finished bottle of wine stood on the edge of the tub.

He was massaging her shoulders.

She asked about her. Who she was. Where they met. "Do you love her?" she said.

"No," he said. "Of course not. We were together in college. We'd lost touch. I thought I was in love with her. And I'd always wondered what would happen if—"

She was crying.

He said, "Shit. I'm sorry. I'm such a fucking idiot."

But she was already turning herself around, maneuvering herself into his lap.

Water and suds sloshed over the edges of the tub, spilling onto the floor she'd slept on after David. A glass shattered on the tile. And then the wine bottle tipped, plunked into the water, and filled the tub with Pinot noir.

• • •

She was making dinner on Friday night. Jim was working late. And while that forced her to breathe into a brown paper bag for a few minutes, she saw an opportunity to spend some time not thinking of anything at all besides bringing water to a boil, dicing vegetables, cracking pasta in half.

He came home as she was piling all of the food onto her plate. He said, "Save some for me?"

She smiled, shoveled half her plate onto the empty one sitting across the table.

She relit the candles she'd blown out before the food was finished cooking.

He said, "Smells great. Haven't had this in a while."

"Me neither."

"What's the occasion?"

"A fresh start."

She kissed him. He poured the wine. And they ate together, asking all the same inane questions they would ask each other back before the world caved in under her feet. Before he was responsible for that cave in. Before he made pleasantries seem absurd, and before she'd found a way for guilt to step in on her end.

After dinner he did the dishes while she gathered the laundry.

She called for him to answer the door when she heard the doorbell over the dryer.

In the kitchen, an armful of clothing, she said, "Who is it?"

Jim said, "No one named Meredith lives here."

She froze. The laundry fell to the floor. And she heard David say, "Who are you?"

Jim said, "I own this house. Who the hell are you?"

She peeked her head around the corner, saw David standing on the porch. Jim, holding the door open, said, "Well? Who are—"

"Meredith?" David said.

She stepped into the foyer listening to her own breathing. The paper bag she'd used earlier was already in the trash. So she counted breaths, made an effort to breathe. Otherwise she was certain she would forget. And collapse. The image of her husband and David checking for signs of life together made her draw in a breath so large it hurt her lungs.

"Who the fuck is Meredith?" Jim said.

She raised her hand.

David's shoulders slumped, made him small, soft.

Jim said, "Meredith. Wasn't that on our list?"

She leaned against the wall. She covered her mouth with her hand.

David said, "There is no Meredith. Is there?"

Her husband answered his question, said, "Not that I know of. I suppose there won't ever be, now." He turned to her, his face contorted, as if he was punched in the gut.

David scratched his head, said, "I'm sorry. I didn't know."

Jim leaned against the door, pinched between his eyes. He said, "It's all right."

David turned, walked through the front yard to his car.

From the foyer she watched David drive away.

She and her husband stood, said nothing.

They stared out the front door until Jim said, "I suppose we're even now, then."

• • •

The following Friday, on the park bench during her smoke break, her friend said, "Are you happy?"

"I don't think that's something I need to be worrying about right now."

"Then what are you thinking?"

"Surviving. Waking up tomorrow, the next day. The day after that. At this point I think happiness is a while away."

"At least you tried, right?"

She ashed her Camel, said, "Yeah. At least."

They finished their cigarettes and went back to work talking about other things.

She got home late. Around the same time she'd found Jim months before. Her breathing was normal, her eyes were dry. She didn't need a paper bag.

The smell of burnt food hit her first as she walked inside. Then it was the sound of Jim cursing, pots clanging against the stove, boiling water bubbling onto the burners.

He was cooking in the kitchen. Or trying to. He said, "Hi."

They finished a bottle of wine. Left the dinner plates at the table unfinished.

They fumbled with each other's clothes. She thought it felt like the first time she'd ever been undressed by another person. Awkward and strange. Alien.

So they took off their own clothes, folded them, placed them into piles next to the bed on their respective sides.

She laid on her back while he propped himself up over her. He did his routine. Her mouth, her neck, her nipples. Then his face was between her legs.

And it stayed there.

She felt nothing.

She said, "This isn't working."

He stood up. She saw that nothing was happening for him either. He said, "Want me to use my fingers?"

"You know that's not what I mean."

Naked, staring at the ceiling, they laid next to each other until he answered a phone call from work, said he had to write an email.

She got up, dressed herself, and went to the kitchen to clean up the mess they'd left from dinner.

I Sing the Body Electric Blue

When you're on what I'm on everything's electric. Little sparks of blue light from your fingertips, the palms of your hands, the ropes connecting your eyeballs to your brain. I could graze the stem of my desk lamp with my finger right now, watch the energy arc from my skin into the metal like zat, zat, zat.

They didn't list this as one of the side effects.

They were right about the nausea, the spins, the lethargy. But not this. Not the minor superpowers.

I say minor because in a world without superpowers even the littlest ones are the most fantastic. And I've got them. And they're wonderful.

My husband, when he asks how I'm feeling I can say words like Great now. Like Tremendous. Like Stupendous.

But I don't. It would be too much. It would feel like lying. Not because those words would be untrue, but because no one goes from hair-tearing, laugh-crying, wall-punching fits to Fantastic in the span of a couple weeks without coming off as a different kind of crazy.

So I say, "Good."

Or, "Fine."

Or, "Calm."

Then I smile without teeth and turn back to the television and pay more attention to the electric pulse behind my belly button, on the tips of my nipples, arcing across the hairs on the back of my neck.

Before, my husband would watch me. I could see him in the corner of my eye thinking, taking mental notes, analyzing. He knew when I was dipping below baseline or rocketing above it. He always said I'd had—he called it an aura. And depending on my trajectory I'd react accordingly.

Overreact accordingly.

I'd turn, show my teeth, ask him what the fuck he was looking at, tell him to read his fucking book, say he should swivel his head around and fuck right off.

Or.

I'd smile, climb into his lap and put my tongue down his throat, unzip his pants and tell him to stand, take off my clothes and ask him what he was waiting for.

Now he watches me sizzle electric blue. I don't even watch him from my periphery because I can feel it in my eyes, the energy. Cool, glowing sapphires. Their reflection in the glass of the fireplace doors, in the momentary black of the television screen before commercial breaks, in the dog's eyes when he wags his tail and yips at me looking like a camera flash went off in his face.

But everything has a price.

You can't feel like you can jump into an electrical socket in Philadelphia and zap yourself to the top of the Empire State Building without side effects to the side effects. But a world that sounds like it's been wrapped in cotton is worth the space between your feet and the floor—that opposing polarity that allows more gliding than walking. The airiness where worry and doubt and pressure and panic used to be is worth the crackling static distance between your body and the mattress that can lull you to sleep. Sleep without the heat in your mouth and the taste of iron in the morning.

Sometimes my husband says my name, asks a question.

But the liquid white light in the overhead supermarket fluorescent bulbs isn't as pure as what's going on with me.

Most nights he tells me about his day.

But the digital numbers in the cable box feel artificial compared to me.

When he says Julie louder and louder in our kitchen I say, "Hmm?"

And he says, "Do you want me to make lemon chicken tonight?"

I smile, no teeth, say, "It doesn't matter."

He says, "I figured I'd make it. You haven't asked for it in a while."

Looking at the floor, the shadow I'm leaving on the laminate tile as my energy keeps me from feeling the cold under my bare feet, I say, "Whatever you want."

He puts his hands on my shoulders, says, "But what do you want?"

I kiss him.

The static shock from my lips makes him jerk his head away.

I say, "It doesn't matter."

We eat together, go to movies together, walk the dog together. In the mornings we work around each other in the bathroom. At work, we text each other. With what I'm on, with the powers I've got, I can fit myself back into our little universe. And I'm happy.

Even when he asks me if I would consider a lesser dosage I'm happy.

With a smile and my new blue eyes, I say, "I don't want to be what I was."

He tells me he loved me then as much as he loves me now. But I'm different.

I zap myself to the splotch of spackle still visible through the new paint.

I change the lighting in the room, bathe it in x-rays, and phase to each spot my fist went through, the holes he was able to patch up better.

I jump into the chandelier, flash out of his alarm clock into our bedroom and point out the new windows. The shatterproof ones.

I dive through the cable wire, blink into the kitchen through the microwave, and show my husband my wrecked knuckles. The places where my hair hasn't grown back all the way just yet. The cracked fingernails that will never heal right.

He's on the verge of tears and my head's cocked to the side and I'm smiling.

My palm on his cheek, I say, "I'm better now. Not better-better, but better than I was."

He's crying now.

I try to show him, channel the energy through my fingertips, let him feel what I do even if it's for a second.

But, my skin on his, there's nothing. No pulse, no electric arc, no vibration. Just wet fingers.

Pulling my hand away, the energy returns. I feel it in my palms, my fingertips, my bellybutton, my nipples, my new blue eyes.

But when I touch his face again, try to make him experience this—the wonder of it—again, there's nothing.

"I'm better now," I say. "I'd show you if I could."

I'd grip him tight, convert our bodies into lighting and use the power lines. I'd take us to the Golden Gate Bridge and the Eiffel Tower and Big Ben and Edinburgh Castle. We'd live outside time and space as comingled energies, and I'd show him what's been done for me, how much better I am. We'd skip up through the sky, cloud to cloud on water droplets. Bounce across the satellites in orbit, disperse ourselves into the atmosphere as light—a phenomenon for history books.

But instead, in our kitchen, I watch him cry.

And no matter what I try, I can't show him how this feels.

How I feel.

This Distance

From across the street, She watches herself take a deep breath.
Watches herself reach for the door handle.
Watches herself take another big, long breath and pull the door open.
The first time this happened—back when She was the woman who just walked into the restaurant, not the one sitting in the car watching (stalking)—She thought the look she'd practiced in the mirror carried over to dinner quite nicely. Clenched jaw. Shoulders back. Chin up. Big smile.
But time has distorted things.
Her being here now is evidence of that on its own, sure. But through the car window, across the street, through the plate glass restaurant window, She watches her old self, her younger self—Then-her actually—fidget. Watches Then-her's eyes dart from table to table, to the bar, to the restrooms.
Then-her looks like she has something to say with no idea how to say it. Looks like she wants to run through the kitchen and out the back door.
Time hasn't changed that feeling a bit. Sitting, watching, She wants to throw the car into the drive, screech down the road and get the hell home. A decade from now. Where She belongs. Not belongs, really, but where She's supposed to be.
Then-her, she tells the host she has a reservation, says her name. Same first with the old last. With all those Italian vow-

els, just about anybody could hear that name without hearing it. Through glass, from a ways away.

Then-her is told she has to wait, that the rest of her party hasn't arrived yet.

It's difficult to forget how much a person's confidence can deflate by being kept waiting. Then-her's shoulders disappear. A decade from now she'll walk around like that more frequently than she'd care to admit.

She watches Then-her order a vodka. What She told her parents—what Then-her is about to tell them—was as rehearsed as her imagined poise. How she was going to say it and what she was going to do after, it was all mapped out in her mind. But waiting to do any of it meant booze. Back home in her own time, it still does.

Then they pull up.

Her father's driving, parking. Her mother's looking herself over in the sun visor mirror. They're talking. Probably about nothing important because nothing much mattered then. They'd succeeded. Raised a kid into an adult into a self-sufficient human with a job and an apartment and a dog. Retired. Got their snowbird home outside of Orlando.

And Then-her is about to blow that all to shit.

The next ten years won't be kind to them. They're not this version of them back home.

Her mother will have to start wearing glasses. She'll put on about forty pounds. Her smoker's cough will get deep, wet, and it'll break out nearly anytime she speaks more than a handful of sentences. Not that they've spoken more than a few words to one another since tonight.

Her father will lose the rest of his hair. And his color—like his lifeforce was sucked out the top of his head by just a couple of words: "I'm in love, Dad. Her name's Julie."

He'll get skinny. Old man skinny. She can't remember him saying anything at all the once or twice they'd seen each other since a few minutes from now.

She can't sit in the car and watch anymore. Here's where She needs to get off her ass and do something.

She's out of the car at the same time they're out of theirs. Walks soft enough that they can't hear her coming up from behind them.

By now, Then-her is finishing her drink. If She can shift the timeline properly, Then-her'll have a second, a third before she realizes her parents aren't coming, that something's come up.

Then-her, she'll be pissed. She'll tell them off in a text. Say that they should've let her know they needed to reschedule before she'd ordered her first overpriced drink. Say that she'll talk to them later after she calms the eff down—she can't curse at her parents yet. Embarrassing.

Then-her, she'll tell them what she needs to tell them another time—when she musters up the strength again. Then maybe she'll put it off another time because the Eagles make the Super Bowl and her father wouldn't be able to concentrate on anything anyhow. Then maybe she'll put it off again because it was too close to her mother's birthday. Again and again until she has to convince Julie to stay with her even though she can't come out because she can't lose them. After that, everything would be okay. Wouldn't be so fucking complicated

Her parents would get to age properly.

Sundays would still come along with an open invitation to dinners at their house.

Turning red on the beach after too much beer would be dealt with summer after summer.

She and Then-her would merge into something new. A person half-bottled up, half-still a daughter. A composite person with a long-term roommate.

They're almost at the door. They're almost reaching for the handle. They're almost going to sit in front of Then-her. They'll leave without saying anything soon.

She reaches for them. Opens her mouth to say she's changed her mind about the restaurant, that they'll go somewhere else. And so what that time travel could unmake the universe? So what that this version of her would be gone? So what that every good thing that's happened despite all the bad things would be erased? Her mother and father don't call her daughter anymore and neither She nor Then-her can live like that. Then-her just doesn't know it yet.

But then time makes sure She can't change anything.

She trips over the curb, falls onto the sidewalk. Time makes sure She lives with knowing her parents are living, but that's all, by scraping her knees to shit. Time makes sure She doesn't live the rest of her life in a paradox loop by breaking her goddamn toe.

Or maybe it's just that things can't be changed. Full stop.

She's still clumsier than hell after all, even with all the Julie-mandated yoga.

Her parents step inside the restaurant, make their way through to their daughter.

In a couple minutes Then-her won't exist. The Person-She-used-to-be will try to fix things a couple times. Try to talk it through. But after a decade or so, She'll be all that's left.

She can't do anything now but limp back to the car, go home, and wait for Then-her to catch up with her. And she will catch up. Eventually.

But for now, She'll watch from the driver's seat for a little longer before heading back where she's supposed to be.

Through the car window, across the street, through the plate glass restaurant window, they're smiling, talking about nothing really.

They're buttering bread, sipping from wine glasses.

They're together and it's good.

And from this distance, they look like they're enjoying themselves.

Yeah? Well My Friend Chris Hemsworth Says You Ain't Shit

When Chris gets a few in him I can't understand a damn word he says. All sawed-off Australian syllables. Oi, oi, oi, and all that, know what I'm saying?

A couple more and he's showing me pictures of his wife telling me I'll never get a woman like that.

I'll say, "Talk American."

And he'll say, "Death and taxes, partner, yeehaw," making sure everyone hears it.

I'll tell him he has a distinct advantage. "You're fucking Thor," I'll say.

Another photo on his phone, and, "No, she's fucking Thor." Then he'll slap the table, laughing, sloshing beer out of our glasses onto our food. He'll stand, flex, say, "You are, all of you, unworthy of the weight of mighty Mjolnir."

As if people wouldn't be staring by then already.

Not only is Thor in a bar, he's drunk and insulting his pudgy American friend in a bar, swearing enough to blush any face in earshot and showing off semi-nudes of a supermodel.

It wouldn't matter that I'd told him he could only have one beer. That it'll be my night. That he'll be my wingman.

Wouldn't matter if he'd said, "Sure, sure. No worries, mate."

I know what that means. He says he calls me mate because we're friends. But when he's shoving me around, grinding his knuckles into my scalp, ranting about my fleeting mortality, it has to be for some other reason. And if I were to tell him it'd be best if he'd just piss on my leg and get it over with, he'd do it, and toss a wallet-full of foreign cash into the air as an apology and a fuck it.

So I'll just let him drink, say, "How about a shot, Odinson?"

Or, "Another round, First Mate Chase?"

Or, "How about some more tequila, Gale?"

He always gets so huffy about his brother landing a major film franchise the same time he did. That everything's always been Liam, Liam, Liam. That his brother deserves a nut like Miley. That he's met Jennifer Lawrence once and she's not even really all that. And after that, he'll skulk to the men's room saying he shouldn't have ordered the clams casino from this pit. Again.

Then it'll be the guilt.

Yeah, Chris is a jerkoff sometimes, but he's my jerk off, you know? Sure, he's sensitive for a man of his stature, but who wouldn't be? The body, the looks, the fame, the supermodel wife. That's all good, but that's all people see. There's more to Chris than that.

I'll be obliged to find the biggest, toughest-looking guy in the dive and tell him, "Hey, you saw my friend Chris, right? He had some nasty shit to say about you, man. I shouldn't even repeat it."

He'd stand, all Brut and tanning lotion, shove me a little, tell me to tell him what the fuck Captain America said.

Then, the smell of Camels and Jäger wafting from Meat's maw, Chris'll say, "Oi," loud enough that even the jukebox'll shut up.

Then he'll tear the place apart. Bottles'll shatter over heads. People'll slide across the bar. Barstools'll explode across people's backs. The only thing missing will be a sepia filter over the scene and a drunken cowboy playing old-timey Wild West piano in the corner.

Once Chris and I are the only ones left standing, once the bartender tells us to get the hell out of there, once Chris registers the groans of his victims as signs of life, he'll lift a whiskey bottle over his head, say, "JR's Bar, I hath had words with thee," and take a good long pull.

When it comes to friendship, all you've got to do is make sure your buddy's good after he gets torn down. Even when you're the one doing the tearing. Chris rips into my ass, I'll spit it all right back in his face, then we'll make it up to each other. Call it practice for the real shit.

We'll both be smiling, all the guilt'll be gone, and we'll walk out of that dump together. Like friends are supposed to.

He'll say, "Come, my doughy American companion, let's go bird-dog some chicks."

"Think I'll flush one out that looks as good as Elsa?" I'll say.

He'll laugh, loud and mighty, say, "Absolutely not, Son of George and Kathy. And keep my wife's name out of your mouth."

Then we'll stagger down the street, arms around each other's shoulders, to go wreck another neighborhood gin joint.

It's Always Something, It's Never Nothing

He's been waiting a while. But he tries to overlook that now.

The sun turns Bridget's hair to gold, makes her teeth white-white. Her ponytail swings left, right, left, right, her breasts bop up, down, up, down every step she takes. The skin showing between her shirt and shorts, the U of her half-exposed belly button. Denim bunching between her thighs.

A bag in one hand, a dog leash in the other, she kicks her head back, says hello even from this distance. Her voice tangles in birdsong and river-flow.

He waves, pats the grass.

They talk a while. Eat the croissants she brought. Play fetch with the dog.

Then they sit, close. Skin against skin.

She talks about how much she's been enjoying the time they've been spending together. Talks about how she wasn't looking for anything to creep up on her so fast. Says, "I wasn't expecting you."

They kiss while the dog gnaws on a bone, while a crew boat paddles by, while joggers' sneakers scrape against the macadam path behind them.

And when she pulls her lips away from his, she smiles, bites her bottom lip—a clump of croissant wedged between her front teeth.

On the walk back to her apartment he asks what sort of Spaniel her dog is.

She says, "He's a mix."

Passing a garbage can on the corner of her street, he points to the balled up bag in her hand, tells her he'll toss it.

She thanks him, drops the white paper ball graying with grease into his hand.

While she shakes her apartment key lose on her ring she burps, loud, deep, wet.

She apologizes, her hand on his chest, her eyebrows arched and crinkling her forehead, cracking her foundation. "That was so gross," she says.

He lies, says no, drags out the end of the word forcing a smile.

It's a nice place. Comfortable, but small. It's been done up nice like she was hoping things would go well enough today for this to happen—but she left out a can of Pledge, left dust on the television stand, overstuffed the closet and pinched clothes between the sliding doors.

It has a smell. Air freshener and dog piss.

She asks him to give her a second, heads into the bedroom alone. Then there's grunting, metal clanging. She says fuck, rams the dog crate into the doorframe.

She says, "Go on in, make yourself at home."

He sits on the bed, picks dog fur off his shorts until the barking stops.

She comes into the room smiling, apologizing for the dog, saying he'll be chewing on a bone for a while.

They roll over onto one another once, twice, three times, all lip gloss and summer breath.

The back of her shirt is damp with sweat. Her bra is wet, leaves red imprints on her ribcage. One of her nipples is inverted—a second belly button.

She smiles straddling him, the hunk of dough still in her teeth.

Once they're both naked, she's hopping up and down on him, hurting him. Air rakes across his vocal cords with every impact, forces gut-punch sounds from his mouth. The slapping gets louder, makes the dog bark and scratch at his cage from the other room.

The dog losing its mind, her nipple an eye magnet, the box spring crackling under the force of them, he tells her to stop, sits up, says, "Maybe—if you—here."

She says, "What?"

He says, "Let's try to—no the other way—yeah, okay."

Behind her, it's nothing but her smell. Jean shorts in summer.

When it's over, side by side, they breathe heavy and smile and tell each other how good the other was. She tells him she hopes she wasn't too much for the first time. He tells her no, no, no, of course not—he liked it. He smiles again trying to ignore the pain in his hips, the soreness in his deflated cock.

On her side, twirling his chest hair around her index finger, she says, "I think I'm falling for you."

He stretches a smile across his face, looks her in the eyes—can't find a single word.

She says, "Nothing?" and smiles—no graying lump of pastry.

"Same," he says. "I feel the same way."

They kiss. Long and wet.

After a bit, her head in the crook of his armpit, her breathing slows, deepens.

And with the sun making the curve of her naked hip glow, and her hair shimmer, and the dust they'd kicked up into the air sparkle, she begins to snore.

Loud.

Like when he used to fake it as a kid when he didn't want to be carted off to school.

He stares at the ceiling a while.

And it's nothing but the nipple, the smell, and where that piece of croissant ended up. Nothing but the aching pain where should be none. Nothing but a lack of whatever people feel when something good happens to them.

But nothing else.

Because it is good. It is.

Stare long enough at clean, white ceiling though and the cracks'll start to show themselves. He follows them with his eyes, watches how they splinter into each other making patterns that can't be painted away.

It's not nothing.

Never is.

It's everything.

• • •

He logs into his bank account on his work computer during his lunch hour. He does it every time he needs to pay a bill, just to be sure. But the number on the screen proves, again, he doesn't need to anymore. Not since he was moved from the cubicle to his office. Not since he got an actual desk. Not since he got his password for the executive network—his last name, first initial, a set of numbers derived from his birthday, month, and year.

He pays all of his bills instead of just the one that's due. Then he leaves his bagged lunch in his mini-fridge, goes down to the cafeteria he'd only heard about from his bosses as they'd walked by his cube saying things like Delicious, and Stuffed, and Better than Sex.

He never returned any of Bridget's texts. Blocked her number after she called four times in a row. After he listened to the messages about how she thought she meant more to him than just a fuck.

At the sushi station, he asks for a Philadelphia roll.

The juice bar, a banana blueberry smoothie.

A slice of coconut custard pie at the dessert counter.

The nice old lady at the register asks him if he'd like a cup for a fountain soda. He smiles, asks for a large.

His bosses—peers—call for him to sit with them.

Michael's teeth match the price of his suit.

David calls him buddy, pulls a chair away from the table.

Bill wipes his glasses with his YSC tie.

They talk about the Eagles, how Jeffrey Lurie is a fantastic businessman, but terrible football franchise owner. They talk about the Sixers, the rotation in which the four of them will divvy up the company's floor seats this coming season. They talk about the new parking passes that are going to be assigned to make sure they all have the spots closest to the elevators in the parking garage.

Then Bill says something about "Filthy fucking liberals."

And Michael says, "Filthy fucking immigrants."

And David says, "Who's coming to the titty bar with me tonight?" He holds up a hand, points to his ring, says something about his wife flying out to LA to visit who-gives-a-shit.

Then it's just the sushi. The chopsticks and the best way to pretend how to use them. The hair coiled on top of cream cheese.

He picks it off and lets the rest of the guys at the table blather on.

He sucks a wad of blueberry from his smoothie into the back of his throat, coughs, sprays his tray with purple. Then he excuses himself from the table, choking through the words. Leaves the pie, film forming on the custard.

The specks of smoothie don't come out of his shirt, leave the white gray with a spot of juice in the center.

He spends the rest of the day taking calls from the marketing department, the customer service specialists, the other executives. Most of them are angry at someone or something, this or that, and he's kind over the phone.

He says, "I apologize for the inconvenience."

And, "We will do better to give you more notice, but really could use the assist this one last time."

And, "Everything will be resolved within the next twenty-four hours, I assure you."

He ignores the notification about his paycheck's direct deposit while he googles breathing exercises for anxiety. While he runs his fingertips in circles on his temples. While he leans back in his chair, sits up straight, breathes and then figures that everything on Google is a crock of shit.

He checks his account just before he heads out for the night.

Another big check. Triple the amount he used to get working in his cube next to Sandra the Foot—the lady who slips off her shoes to air-out her corns. Next to the men's room that Stankin' Franklin would destroy every day after lunch. Across the hall from Reality Anne who would use up most of her day reading celebrity gossip sites only to email links of nip-slips and viral videos to everyone on the team.

He passes them as he heads to the elevators.

He smiles, says goodnight.

No one says anything.

In the elevator, David calls him buddy again, says, "So? Titty bar?"

"I think I'm coming down with something. Going to take it easy tonight."

"Come on, don't be a bitch. You aren't even married."

He fakes a smile, says that's true, asks what club David'll be haunting.

"Platinum Penthouse, out in the burbs. Gets pretty wild. Good thing we just got paid, know what I mean?"

A deep breath, a five count, an exhale.

And in his car, leaving the parking garage, he gets on the westbound side of the highway trying to keep up with David's tail lights speeding away.

• • •

The first beers go down fast and the women start calling him baby faster.

He mimics David, crumples up dollar bills at the stage and aims for asses. Smokes cigarettes for the first time since college, hacking, gagging a little. Taps shot glasses onto the bar before throwing them back, trying to push through the burn without beer so David stops calling him bitch.

They sit in plush seats in front of the stage.

He watches David slip money into dental-floss-thin underwear, toss clumps of it into the air, pinch bills between his teeth for the girls to take from him with their breasts.

He tries to keep up. Fails.

Peaches, nude and shimmering, plops herself onto his lap, pulls the cigarette from his lips, smokes it, blows it in his face, and says, "How about a dance?"

In the backroom, she shows him her piercings. All of them.

She leaves glitter all over his suit coat, her breath in his nostrils.

Back at the stage, a stripper calling herself Lust drains his beer, tells him he could get a dance with her and Brazil at only twice the price.

He's only ever seen what the two of them do to each other inches from his face on the internet. But they make *When Harry Met Sally* sounds. Rehearsed and laughable.

At the bar, David says strippers aren't people. Not really. Gave their humanity away when they took this job. He says, "You're too timid, man. You need to let go. Enjoy yourself. They're here. Use them."

He doesn't tell David to fuck himself.

Doesn't finish his beer and leave David with the bill.

He pretends to laugh, says he'll try, and orders a beer for himself and his boss—colleague.

It doesn't go down as fast anymore. Tastes more like ash light beer. Gets warm in his hand while he waits for David to come back from the Champagne room.

A woman—tattooed, called Phee—sits next to him, says something about a long face.

He says, "Hmm?"

She says, "Not having fun?"

"Oh, no, sure I am. Lots of fun."

She tucks a rope of purple hair behind her ear, smiles, says, "You look really nice, you know that? Not like the other guys that come in here."

He knows that's not true, not anymore, says, "Yeah? Why's that?"

"Just have a feeling."

She leans in, puts her lips to his ear, says, "I'll cheer you up in the bathroom for two hundred bucks."

And then it's David standing between them telling Phee not to give—he calls him This Guy—any attention. He says, "How about you, me, and that smackable ass of yours get some Champagne?"

Phee and David walk off giggling, leaving him to his warm beer and stack of singles.

He doesn't see David again.

Phee is left out of the on-stage line-up.

And when the lights come up a bouncer taps his shoulder, calls him Buddy, tells him it's time to go.

So he goes.

To his car.

To his apartment.

To bed.

Only to stare at the white ceiling he can't see in the dark.

• • •

His mother's the only person with his new number.

The phone is more toy than anything else. Came in a bubble package glued to a cardboard sleeve.

He told her he was going away for a while.

She said, "Where?"

He named a place she'd heard of before.

She said, "Why?"

He told her whatever she wanted to hear.

She said, "Have you ever even gone camping before?"

He lied, said of course.

As he hammers the last tent peg into the ground, checks the instructions just to be sure he's not missing something, she texts, says she's just making sure he that he made it.

He tells her he's where he wants to be.

The sun splintering into spotlights through the trees is better than his office. The static of water rushing over rock is more pleasant than the nasty voicemails left for him by David, and Michael, and Bill. The birds peeping across the caverns between branches, squirrels using piles of leaves as crash pillows, and— the quiet.

Different than the silence in his apartment. The non-sound.

This isn't loneliness. It's solitude. A thesaurus of elegant alternatives to Alone.

He laughs, can almost see the sound waves ping-pong from tree bark to rock ledge to exposed roots and back into his head.

He's nothing but Whitman walking, naming trees and rocks, marking them for later so he can get back to his car.

Eventually.

He props his pack up at the side of the tent, builds a fire in front once the wind catches a chill. He tosses more wood on to the flames once the light fades. And when the fire stops warming all of him he wraps himself in a blanket to keep his back warm.

The pot of baked beans doesn't cook right. A layer of Pam didn't stop a brown crust from embedding itself in the metal's atoms. The top layer of beans is cold.

But he eats everything he could slop into a bowl, fills the pot with water and his backup bar of Irish Spring. He still has a pan for his eggs, but the other cans of beans would go to waste. He wouldn't eat them at home.

He never really liked baked beans anyway.

The inside of the tent does nothing but shift in the wind. Vinyl scraping against metal poles that attacks the space where his skull meets his spine. Nails on a chalkboard—only ever done in movies and by kids after watching stupid movies.

He can't sleep.

Doesn't.

Every snapping twig or shifting pile of leaves pops his eyelids open so he can stare at nothing but black. And the world is black. Not like three in the morning at the apartment with the digital clock across the room, the street lamps through the window, the text messages waking up his phone. This is the void. What death is, maybe.

Death is supposed to have that tunnel at the end, though. That's what people say. A speck of white that expands into a lone headlight into an opening into—whatever.

There's no tunnel.

Just sounds.

Something ripping, tearing on the other side of a millimeter-thick sheet of bullshit pulled over a wire skeleton.

His pack. His food. Everything he brought left outside. He blames himself this time, not Google. He'd read something about hanging his food from trees or keeping it in a cooler in his tent.

But he does nothing now.

Can't do anything now.

He waits until the thing snacking on his peanut butter cracker sandwiches and his toothpaste and his allergy medicine drags the rest of his pack away into the night before he moves anything but his eyes. Then he sits, stares into the space between his folded legs—a heart of tent floor. All jagged, fleshy and hairy around the edges as the sun comes up. The more light that burns through the tent, the more his heart numbs his legs, the more the rising temperature makes him smell himself through his boxer-briefs.

Get close enough to anything, it stinks.

• • •

The sound down the river a ways makes him hide behind a tree to strip. Frantic, jerky movements. He'd laugh if the waterfall didn't remind him of highway sounds. If he didn't feel the need to scramble from the tree to the water, his dick and balls flopping, afraid someone from a car window would point, laugh.

But there's no highway.

No cars zigzagging through the trees.

No people to watch the show.

But he curses anyway. He calls the water temperature a motherfucker, knee-deep. He calls the whatever stole his shit in the night a cocksucker while the water flows into his belly button. Bill and Michael and David a pack of assholes. Bridget a clingy bitch. His mother a meddler. The sky, looking up, drifting through the water, a—sight.

Light blue with wisps of white.

He takes a breath.

Closes his eyes.

Lets the air go.

Then he rights himself, plants his feet into the sludge under the water.

He doesn't recognize the trees. Can't find his clothes pile, the scrape marks in the leaves where his feet dragged through.

He turns and turns and turns.

Until there they are.

He has to squint, stand facing the current.

Laughing, he didn't mean the things he said. Not any of it.

But maybe he did.

A little.

Widening his stance, spreading his arms, he lets the river wash away his stink. Or at least replace it with the water's nickel.

He has to take a step back. Then another. And another.

Keeping himself standing makes his breathing heavy. Makes his forehead pimple with beads of sweat. Makes him angle himself toward the bank. Makes the volume of the falls a ways away behind him increase. Maybe. He could be hearing things out of, what, fear. Seeing things because of, probably, nerves.

Like when he searches for visible pores on a beautiful woman's face.

Or dredges for the deepest, blackest shit inside people searching for reasons to walk.

But it could be that that's what's called settling. Sticking with awful things until they're not so bad, until they're sort of nice.

He leans back, feels the water take him, stares at the sky.

The sun dries the water on his chest. His exposure stiffens him a bit. The sounds of the falls get louder, deeper, more intense.

He kicks his legs, spins through the water, feels it beating his hair to his head.

And then it's the sky.

The sun.

The mist-white haze.

Through the light bouncing off the water in the air, there's nothing to see but bright.

He watches, floats, drifts.

He'll wait another second to right himself. To stand, head for the bank.

Another second.

And another second.

And another.

Embracing Skeletons

Cory says Jessica is pissed. At me, at Ben. But mostly me.

Leaning against the bar, waiting for our beers—paid for in part by his parents—Cory says, "You should have told us earlier," and peeks over his shoulder.

Jessica's across the room, smiling, laughing. Hugging and kissing friends and family hello.

"I had nothing to do with this," I say. "It was all Ben."

"Yeah, well. Shit."

"Really, I had no clue what was coming. I don't think he did, either. His job—"

"I get it." Cory thanks the bartender for his beer, takes a drink. "When you guys—if you guys get married—keep in mind I owe you a no-call, no-show."

Cory opens his mouth, but Sara shows up, silences the room. She announces herself with an "I made it," and a "Woo-Woo," while she raises the roof and asks if anyone knows who made up that dumbass move. Then it's all mussed hair and bullshit about getting lost. "This city is like *Labyrinth* without Bowie," she says. Then she points at me, "He did call to say he wants his pants back, though."

I yell across the room, say I wasn't the one who bought them. But no one hears me. I say it's Ben's fault. But I can't hear myself over the guests and the bridal party laughing.

Cory talks about Ben again. Says Jessica still expects a gift. Asks if I'm fucking up another relationship. Or fucking other guys. Again.

Sara butts in, slaps Cory on the back, tells him to relax.

"You're in trouble, too," Cory says. "Don't let Jess get you alone. Unless of course you want to be me. Fair warning, Me sucks right now." He curses, excuses himself, mingles.

Sara orders a beer, a shot, slaps a credit card on the bar before the bartender can tell her the liquor's not included. She says, "Keep it open."

After the tequila grimace she says, "Where's Ben?"

"Where's Jordan?"

She flips me her undecorated ring-finger.

"What happened?"

"I showed you mine. Show me yours, bitch."

"Mutual thing."

"It's never mutual. But if we're playing it that way, same here. What'd you tell the happy couple?"

"Ben's away on business."

"Shit, I used that one too." She slaps my shoulder, laughs. "Think they think we're canoodling behind the backs of our significant others?"

"Together? No. And gross. But, probably."

We drink together until the buffet opens. Sara kisses my cheek, tells me to get laid, then goes to make a plate.

I watch her say hello to people in kisses and hugs. Her conversations last just long enough to leave an impression. But she doesn't give anyone enough time to ask her why she's alone.

While she eats I can't decide if I'm more jealous of her ability to keep food down or fake a smile.

I order beer, drink it, order another.

I lose track of Sara when my stomach turns on me.

Glossy skin, the shakes. Sitting or standing depending on how and when my guts flop over.

The party is all selfies and group shots.

It's Cory and Jessica smiling, kissing.

It's me in the background, skin a shade of bone.

Then it's Jessica next to me. A sneer, all teeth and a set of eyes. "Did you and Sara plan this?" she says.

"Hmm?"

"Ben? Jordan?"

"Ready for tomorrow? I heard your dress is beautiful."

"Stop. And it is, thank you. But, seriously? Do you know what no-shows do to a seating chart?"

"Make for more leg room?"

Jessica's face softens a little. There's almost a smile. "Does Ben think you're funny? Because I don't think you're funny."

"Businessmen like him don't usually get my humor. Friends do though." I swallow hard, show my teeth.

She pats me on the back, says, "Why don't you come hang out with us instead of sitting here all night? I think Cory could use you. He's freaking out a little."

"Not feeling a hundred percent."

"No, really?" Jessica rubs my back, says, "Feel better, okay? Just because I'm pissed off doesn't mean I want you dead."

I swallow again, stare past Jessica, blink away a wet tingle in my eyes. Say, "What about Ben?"

"Right now?" she says. "Let's just say he's lucky the death penalty's illegal in Rhode Island." Then she winks, turns and walks away.

I wave to the bartender, put up a finger, tell him to put it on Sara's tab.

The shot burns. But not the good way.

My guts gurgle. I sit, stand, wipe sweat from my face with pulpy napkins, think of what puke does to an already wrecked esophagus.

Next time I'm up, I stay up.

There's a cadence to my drunk. A step, a dragged foot, a hip to a table, an apology. Repeat.

It's my shoes scraping across the linoleum bathroom floor, the grind of the stall door's hinges.

Then it's a guy on the toilet, Sara's head in his lap.

She turns, wipes away runny eye makeup, says, "What? Like you haven't done this before?"

I kick my way into the next stall, splash the toilet with booze.

The other guy's cursing. Asking why Sara's crying. Asking if he's done something wrong.

I wish the tile floor was cooler. I ask the walls if people can get sick from vomit-to-skin contact. "It wasn't on any of the lists," I say. "I can't remember what the doctor said."

It's Sara telling the guy nothing's wrong and apologizing for me.

It's the guy asking if she's sure she's alright over and over, then leaving.

Then it's me and Sara on the bathroom floor putting me back together.

• • •

Sara cleans me up, walks me to the hotel. She tucks me in, kisses my forehead, leaves.

But Cory won't let me sleep.

He keeps texting, keeps asking me to meet him at the bar once the rehearsal ends. It's, "Please," at ten thirty-six, then, "Come on, dude," at eleven thirteen. By midnight he's misspelling curse words. And just before one I'm at the bar ordering a Shirley Temple—I'd heard soda settles stomachs.

"This is all—this is all crazy, right?" Cory says.

"Big day tomorrow."

"That's not what I mean."

"What, nerves? Everybody gets nervous."

"Do you ever get nervous about you and Ben?"

"Don't you think it's about time you get some sleep?"

He orders more to drink, says, "Tomorrow, right? I'm going to smile, and everything'll be perfect. And I'll look like I belong there. But I don't know if I belong there. I'll have to pretend. I'll have to act."

"I think everybody has to act a little sometimes."

"Yeah, well. You're really bad at it."

"What's that?"

"You're acting." He hiccups, says, "You're lying about something. And you're terrible at it."

"Yeah? And you're a shitty drunk."

Cory stares.

I sip my soda, wince.

He says, "What's going on? Tell me or I leave." He pulls his car keys from his pocket, twirls them on his finger. "I'm drunk enough to walk away from this whole thing, I swear." Then he stands, tells me I'm a terrible actor. He talks about my sweating. My shivering. That people thought it was weird that I sat by myself all night and left with Sara.

"It's nothing," I say. "I'm here alone. I'm upset about it."

"Fuck it." Cory turns, leaves the bar, walks through the hotel lobby. And once he reaches the door, he runs.

I'm on cement legs. They grind over the lobby's polished tile, they scrape the concrete outside. For each step forward a foot drags behind. But I listen for Cory's jangling car keys a ways ahead and follow.

I'm sweating everywhere. My face. My chest. My ass cheeks, greasy with every stride. In the valet circle, I'm choking down humidity. A pull, a swallow, a gasp. My palms leave sweaty prints on my knees.

Then Cory runs past saying he can't find the fucking parking lot.

I lunge, wrap my arms around his hips. We collapse into a pile of limbs. All "Get the fuck off me," and "Fucking stop it," and other assorted nastiness.

It's an elbow—maybe a knee—that mashes my nose flat.

Then it's me crab-walking away, kicking my legs and dragging my ass across the sidewalk. I'm catching blood in my free hand, cursing as it slops onto my shirt.

Cory says, "Oh, fuck."

I say, "Jessica's going to be so pissed if it's broken."

And Cory tells me to let him take a look.

I tell him I'll take care of it, say, "Get the fuck away from me."

Cory keeps coming, and I start yelling.

Then I'm on my feet, keeping space between us. I hold up my clean hand, say, "Seriously. Fucking stop."

And he does.

But he apologizes, stares at my shirt, the blood seeping from between my fingers.

I say, "It's fine. I just don't want to ruin the pictures."

He keeps staring, saying, "Sorry. I'm so sorry."

The red shirt Ben bought for me, the one I'm wearing—seems my blood can ruin everything now.

• • •

I'm picking dried blood from my nostrils past two in the morning.

Every used, blood-soaked, brown-speckled tissue—and the shirt Ben loved me in—is dropped into a plastic bag. The bag is tied off in double, triple, quadruple knots, and stuffed in the bottom of my suitcase.

I Google biohazard disposal methods. Research if it's tossed in a landfill. Or burned. Stuffed down abandoned coals mines. Or fired off into space.

I imagine archeologists a thousand years from now finding it, exposing themselves to it, being the inadvertent destructors of all future human life.

Cory stays a bit. Sits on my bed asking questions. How long I've known. How it happened. Who it happened with. What I told Ben—if I told Ben.

I tell him I'm tired, that he needs to get to bed too.

His eyes drift to all the bags in the room. The one in the corner, unopened. Another on its back, guts spilled out. A duffel on the armchair. A canvas shopping bag stuffed with books, lying on its side on the desk.

He says, "Why'd you pack so much stuff?"

I lay on the bed, say, "Choices."

"Couldn't decide on something?"

"No, I decided."

Then he leaves like he knows. Or at least he's pretending to know what I did before coming here. At the very least he knows there's no fucking business trip.

I turn onto my stomach when the door closes behind him.

My pillowcase is wet when Sara knocks saying it's her through the door.

I let her in. She says hey, tromps inside, throws her purse and herself onto my bed.

"Why's your face all red?" she says.

"Cory and I were wrestling."

"Don't tell Jessica."

Lying on her stomach, her head propped up in her hands, she apologizes. She kicks her legs up at the knees. Right leg, she's sorry about what I saw in the bathroom. Left leg, she's sorry she didn't tell me about Jordan earlier. Both, she says, "You know how I get when I'm upset."

"Really, it's fine," I say. "Sorry for the whole vomit thing. Sorry I ruined your date."

"Shut up."

I smile, say, "That's where you've been, isn't it."

"You shouldn't question the person who got you back here alive."

I don't say anything. But I turn away.

She says, "That came out wrong." Then she says nothing until she asks if she can stay the night.

"My nose was bleeding," I say. "I might—"

"Please just let me." Her sentence catches in the back of her throat. She sucks back something wet, wipes her eyes.

I lay on my back next to her.

We stare at the ceiling. *Friends* on the television. Bad jokes and laugh tracks. Me, an exposed nerve pulsing.

Sara rolls onto her side to face me. I roll, face her.

She takes my hand.

I say, "No," try to pull it away.

She tells me to stop, kisses it.

I say something else, but it comes out syllables. All broken and whiney. But Sara presses herself into me, says, "Shh."

"I need to tell you some stuff," I say. "I need to tell a lot of people some stuff."

"Shh."

We fall asleep like that.

And I dream of Embracing Skeletons.

• • •

This Distance

The bridesmaids have to hold their dresses down in the wind. A handful of steps into the ceremony and it's already red faces and thong underwear.

Jessica emailed before the sun came up with all the day's particulars. She told us not to get too crazy before boarding the Bridal Party Trolley. "Not" was in caps. The trolley became the BPT after its first mention. "Watch Cory's intake, groomsmen. Can't have a sloppy groom," was in italics. Then a threat was issued that made me picture her as a spiked-backed lizard in a wedding dress burning down Providence.

Meticulous detail and specific instructions, all ruined by the wind forcing whitecaps on Mount Hope Bay. Forcing the tie out of my suit coat. Forcing wives in the congregation to cover their husband's eyes.

But it cools my neck. The drizzle doesn't hurt, either—but I swear I hear it sizzling off my skin.

The bridesmaids walk down an aisle made of grass and white plastic chairs. They mouth apologies to anyone who caught the free show.

And I think of acid rain.

I've heard it's harmless in a mist like this. Not concentrated enough. But if it comes just a bit harder it could stain clothes, sting eyes. Then Jessica would regret including "Rain or Shine" on the invites.

My attention drifts from the bridesmaid procession, crosses the bay to a gray splotch in the sky. It rolls toward us in shapes. A rabbit, fluffed up and holding a pocket watch. An elephant, fat and flying with its ears. Then there's a face. Human enough, open-mouthed and widening until it eats its own self in reverse.

Then everything's just rain clouds. A shade of gray that suggests more than a threat. A promise.

There's a camera flash. Photographers fan out across the ceremony to capture everything.

Everything except the coming clouds.

The bridesmaids are careful walking on the soft lawn. Their free hands ready for another gust off the bay. But Sara—bringing up the rear—walks like she doesn't give a fuck. A stride faster than the others, having to pause every other step so she doesn't flat-tire the bridesmaid in front of her. She grins, rolls her eyes, makes faces at me. She tries to get me to crack a smile, let a chuckle slip.

But I couldn't laugh at Sara's Jessica impression during breakfast at the hotel. Her glory hole joke on the BPT would have been funny, and true, before my results came in. And never mind the wind, she'd stand over a fan and pose like Marilyn Monroe for the minister if she thought it would make me laugh.

She should know better by now.

But she's trying. So I pretend.

The bridesmaids line up on their side on the pergola. On our side, we stand with our hands folded in front of our balls. And it's all privates for me as Jess begins her walk up the aisle.

Another flash.

It's Jessica in white.

It's all of us dressed up, smiling. Or pretending to.

It's Jessica's father opening an umbrella over his daughter as the rain picks up a bit.

And me, hoping the rain doesn't melt the makeup I caked over the rash crawling up my face.

On the girls' side, Sara stares at me. No silliness. No faces. Just a pair of sad eyes.

I stand up straight, show my teeth, hope it looks like a smile.

And then the storm blows its load on us.

• • •

I watch people watch Jessica. Even under the umbrella she looks like she tore herself out of a bridal magazine. Friends point and smile despite the rain. Family members cry as she passes holding programs over their heads. Cory cries under the dripping vines hanging from a wicker archway.

Then it's those vines, plastic, waxy. Hung for a picture.

Zoom in too much, they're flawed, riddled with thorns the frame they were pulled from left behind. Bet they wouldn't wilt if I were to touch them.

Jessica's father gives her away, hands the umbrella to the minister.

I shook her father's hand this morning, said hello. We talked a bit. It was afterward that I held my fingers to my face, checked for micro-tears in the trenches of my fingerprints. Poked my fingertips into my nostrils, looked for flecks of red on my nails.

But blood can't soak through skin, just like acid raid can't liquefy a person.

Funny thing, the imagination, once it realizes the body it's stuffed in is toxic.

Now, in the rain, as Cory cries, as the minister jabbers, as Jessica tries to keep from blinking so as to not fuck up her makeup, I see the umbrella burn away. Skin melt from bones—candle wax dragging a trail. From the tops of their heads, Jessica and Cory's skin rips itself from their skulls in wet sheets.

They're blackened skeletons choking through wedding vows, kissing. Two sets of teeth clattering together, making it all official. The melting crowd applauds.

Then it's over. Each groomsman gives his arm to a bridesmaid.

When it's my turn I have to hold onto Sara's elbow.

A camera flash.

It's me and Sara talking through smiles, heading into cocktail hour.

It's us in line for the bar, me standing with my chest puffed out pretending I feel fine.

It's me whispering to Sara, telling her I'm going to be sick.

In the men's room, I sit on a toilet while my sweat speckles the floor. While I try to figure out what's going to happen first. Or what I'm going to do if both happen at once.

A door opens, all laughter and happiness. Cory calls my name, says, "We've got pictures."

"I look like shit."

"Need me to stall?"

"No. Just stay here for a minute."

I count my breaths, stand, begin to dress.

Then I nearly ruin my pants by not being able to rip them down fast enough.

• • •

After pictures the DJ gives us a ten minute warning before the reception starts.

Sara asks what we're going to do. "Got to make an entrance," she says.

"Whatever you want."

"Come on. We can't be lame."

"We won't be lame."

"We might be."

The bridal party lines up in the order printed in the programs. Me and Sara, we're last.

Sara says, "Fuck this," grabs my arm, drags me to the women's room.

She stuffs our bodies in a space meant for one. She pulls off her dress, tells me to strip.

I say, "What? No."

"Shut up," she says. She pulls my jacket off me, my shirt, tosses her dress in my face. She takes down my pants for me.

I'm pulling the dress over my head when she tells me I'm skinny.

"You too," I say.

"That's not what I mean." She runs her fingers over my ribcage. Bones pressing through wax paper.

We don't say anything after that. We fix ourselves up. The DJ turns on the music, starts calling names. Sara takes my hand, tells me to come on. Then she kicks open the bathroom door when our names are called.

A crowd always cheers for a man in a dress.

There's a flash.

It's me smiling as Sara leads.

Another flash.

It's the dress twirling as Sara spins me.

Another.

It's us acting happy.

After our routine, once the cheering dies down, the DJ introduces Mr. and Mrs. Cory and Jessica Stanton for the first time.

The whole place is standing, watching them dance.

Lights hang from the tent's scaffolding, everything lit for photos. It's all smiles and camera flashes.

Me in Sara's dress.

Sara in my suit.

Cory in tears.

And Jessica wearing a stock-photo face.

It's perfect, and goofy. Memorable as hell with a tinge of shambles.

The rest of bridal party is invited to dance.

Sara and I sway to the music. My muscles spasm. Sara tells a joke tries to get me to laugh when she feels them.

I tell her my sweat's gluing her dress to my skin.

She kisses my cheek, says she already pitted the thing up anyway.

We dance. Her head on my shoulder. My jaw in her hair.

She says, "Everyone's so happy right now."

I say, "Yeah."

"If they knew, you know?"

"Yeah."

• • •

I cut into my steak when dinner's served, but figured I could spare myself by just cramming it into the toilet.

Sara asks if I want another drink, and I ask her about the Pope's hat.

People talk. I react according to their facial expressions.

Cory stops by, squeezes my shoulder.

Sara holds my hand under the table, goes on drink runs before I have the chance to stand.

I smile, I laugh, I drink.

But I'm acid in the rain. I'm lead in the drinking water. I'm mud in the pipes.

The wait staff clears my plate, asks if I found anything dissatisfactory about the food. I say no, smile, sip from my drink.

I smell Sara on me. Her perfume's clinging to me even though we've already changed back into our own clothes. I tell her I smell like her now.

She says, "Yeah, and I smell like you." She sniffs her dress and makes a face.

I'm stink on shit.

I'm out of my seat during her apologies. She doesn't follow me.

I walk the perimeter of the tent. Away from body heat and laughter, the sound of people talking. But the music follows me, drowning the sound of the pouring rain a foot or two away. A song about this being the best day of my life.

There are never any dance songs written about the worst fucking thing imaginable. About stupidity. About death. Where the beat is more a dirge than anything else.

At the bar I order two, tip heavy so the bartender does the same. Over the bottles displayed on the table, just above the tree line, the clouds turn black.

The photos will be on Facebook soon. All kisses and wedding cake. All smiles and dramatic candid moments. But just off the edges of all that is a storm. Acid rain beating on a big white tent, melting it away slow. Water soaking the ground, killing the grass without any of us knowing.

But no one cares. This is a wedding. And a photo tells a thousand lies.

I finish one drink, order another. My throat still burns. Dull and distant.

The DJ plays "Footloose."

I'm double-fisting while two-stepping. I dance with Jessica. She's posing as she dances, waits for the camera flashes.

Then she gets cryptic. Says she knows, that Cory told her.

I turn away to dance with Cory's mom.

I'm sweating through songs, watching water fall from my face. My shirt pastes itself to my chest.

Cory taps my shoulder, keeps in step with me.

Flash, another photo for the album.

It's me and Cory smiling just before he asks me about Ben. Again.

I get a mouthful of ice, drop a cup, watch it explode on the floor. People laugh at the fun drunk dancing.

Then there's Sara. She does "The Twist" with me.

More flashes.

It's Sara kissing me. It's her saying, "I'm sorry. I'll get better with this." It's us dancing until we're in the middle of a ring of bodies.

People have their phones out. They're taking pictures, filming us grinding our asses together. They'll upload open-mouthed smiles, and laughter heard in still frames.

They clap, hoot when the music stops. Even louder when the DJ asks them to give it up for the bridal party once again.

And then I'm lying on the floor. Gin and ice all over.

There's gasping. An "Oh my God," and a, "He just collapsed."

No flashes, but I see spots.

Sara's on her knees saying my name. Cory's calling for everyone to give me room. And Jessica dirties her dress kneeling on the dance floor next to me. Her fingers are on my neck, she's asking me if I hit my head. She says, "We should call an ambulance."

Cory says, "Call Ben."

I say, "Don't."

Sara says, "We have to tell Ben."

It's the three of them hovering over me.

It's the looks on their faces.

And it's me on the floor saying, "Don't tell Ben anything."

Drag

First, it's heat. Blacktop rubbing against clothes, clothes rubbing against skin. Then it's skin peeling off in tiny white rolls. Layer, layer, a third, fourth. Then blood. A trail of it on the road.

The chain doesn't make a sound, pulled taught, clamped to a trailer hitch. It pinches off the windpipe, eats further into skin the louder the engine gets. The more red, pink, and white left behind.

It's the spots, next. Bursts of light, stars in the periphery. It's one, two, four, eight. A thousand. And they're all getting bigger, more intense. Old-timey camera flashes popping, crackling now. Now. Now, now.

The pain stops, but the screaming keeps on keeping on. Gulps of air mixed with exhaust, bits of the road. There's the feeling of spitting that shit out, vocal cords grinding, lungs voiding. But there's no sound over the macadam erasing kneecaps, beer gut, ball sack and hips. Just a raw damn throat and an image of rubber shavings on college ruled paper.

Hands are mostly red strings and bone. But they go at that chain like they could unknot the atoms holding the fucker together. Busted nails, crooked fingers, none of it matters. The chain's going to break. The truck'll get smaller as it speeds up from the lack of drag. People will stop, ask if they can help, call an ambulance, get off their asses and goddamn do something. They'll say, "It's amazing you're alive."

Or, "Jesus, how did you keep your wits about you?"

Or, "Grace under pressure, man. Fucking grace under pressure."

And what else is there to say than, "Once I regained control of the situation, it was nothing." A gummy smile, face all blood and exposed bone.

But no one can unmake a chain with their bare hands.

No one can stop four hundred some horses by digging their heels into the street and wishing.

No one can change anything when shit's this bad.

But eventually it'll be over.

Eventually there'll be nothing.

Life/Hack

Parker Chandler wrote himself into the sequel of his first novel. He broke the news on his Twitter feed. "I decided it was time that I met my monsters. Fuck Mary Shelley."

Two thousand miles away, in a Hactivate bunker, Stanley "H-100" Marks got an H-Mail message from H-0 telling him to activate the Last Straw Protocol.

Stanley did what he was told.

His message hit every H-Directorate device in the continental United States.

Stanley's black computer screen displayed H-Squad's response in green letters. "Thy will be done."

He said, "Fucking-A right, it will."

Then he signed into Netflix to finish *Daredevil* before spoilers hit the fan sites.

• • •

Parker Chandler was a no-show for his reading at the Free Library of Philadelphia.

His agent, Cornelius Maxwell, made the announcement on the library's front steps.

The riot made the ten o'clock news. Fans in full Hactivate cosplay fatigues were caught on camera throwing Molotov cocktails through windows, flipping cars, screaming the Motto into bullhorns.

Reporters were terrified relaying the scene into their foam-tipped microphones. They said, "Fans of controversial novelist, Parker Chandler, have taken to the streets," and "All I can say is this is a scene straight out of a Chandler novel," and, "Holy fucking shit, run."

That one went viral.

Stanley had the message boards on ParkerChandlerWrites.com on auto-refresh. He read posts about Chandler turning to chickenshit because of the impending release of *Hactivate 2* and the vitriolic fan reactions regarding his artistic choices. About Chandler killing himself because if he'd gone nuts enough to write himself into a sequel of the best book in history he was crazy enough to eat a bullet. About how it was all reminiscent of the time he just up and disappeared, let rumors of his death billow up for a while, and came back with a new book ready for his publisher.

There was nothing about a possible kidnapping. About Chandler being chloroformed and tossed into a van. About being blindfolded and interrogated about why he'd found himself in such a situation.

Stanley was given point on this one. He would be the only one to disseminate that information. And he'd do it the right way. The Hactivate way.

He logged into the Hactivate server, keyed in, ETA? Waited.

Green letters. 1930.

He smiled, typed, Whose will be done? Waited.

He loved this part. Got hard thinking about the power he'd been given. Thought of his fan fiction. His hacks. The amount of content he'd pushed onto the internet.

His fingers hovered over his keyboard shaking.

Thy will be done in green.

Stanley logged off the server and left the room.

He had to take three capfuls of ZzzQuil to fall asleep.

• • •

The new recruits were named Nobody, Anonymous, and Nothing. H-110 introduced them all to Stanley, slapped them each across the face.

Stanley never had Greenies sent to his bunker before. Newbs, sure. But Greenies?

He sure as shit wasn't going to question why they were there. Not out loud, anyway. He'd do some reading. Study the Greenie Gun Policy. Practice the ceremony in his quarters. He'd do everything right.

He stared a while, had to force his face slack underneath the single hanging light bulb.

Dressed in gray jumpsuits cinched at the waist with rope, the Greenies stood and stared back, their hands at their sides, balaclavas pulled up to show their faces.

Anonymous shifted his weight from his right foot to his left, the concrete scuffing a bit under his shoes.

Stanley pointed.

H-110 flicked Nobody in the balls with the back of his hand.

Nobody let go of the air in his lungs, closed his lips and let the raspberry fart across the concrete room.

"Confused?" Stanley said, staring at Anonymous.

Anonymous said, "Yes, sir."

H-110 moved to Nothing, readied his hand.

Stanley cleared his throat, stopped H-110.

"Have you read the novel, Anonymous?" Stanley said, forcing the quiver from his voice by increasing the volume at the end of his sentence.

"Yes, sir. I did, sir."

"Mmhm. Are you sure?"

"Yes, sir."

"Then what is there to be confused about?"

Under the pale light of the bulb, Stanley stepped forward. Kept stepping forward. Then he pressed the tip of his nose to Anonymous', felt a drop of sweat slide onto his skin, curl under his nostril, fall to the floor, uncertain whose it was.

He almost blinked, almost averted his eyes.

Then Anonymous said, "I saw the movie, sir."

"Get his ass out of here."

Stanley backed away.

H-110 punched Anonymous in the face. The crackle of shattering nose forced Stanley to turn, gag. He counted to ten trying to ignore the whimpering. He waited until H-110 dragged Anonymous up the wooden steps, opened and closed the door.

Stanley took a breath, waited until his lunch slid back down to his stomach.

He turned, said, "The Moto."

Together, Nothing and Nobody said, "We hack because the world must be hacked. The world must be hacked because no one will hack it for us. Once the world has been hacked we will be free."

"Again."

"We hack because—"

Stanley's phone rang. Starbuck from *Battlestar Galactica* saying frak me over and over. "Excuse me," he said.

Over the phone HS-1 said, "We're here, sir. We're bringing the package to you now."

Stanley swallowed. Hard. Said, "Excellent."

Then he pulled on his balaclava, turned, said, "Well?"

Nothing and Nobody scrambled to pull their masks down.

The basement door opened. A series of sentences echoed down the steps. "Fucking lift," and "I'm going to fall down the goddamn steps, man," and "His shoe came off."

When Stanley cleared his throat, said gentlemen, the guys on the stairs shut up right quick.

He let his smile take him under his mask.

It was grunts and heavy breathing after that until the H-Squad placed the package at Stanley's feet.

Stanley's voice cracked when he said, "Greenies." But it held up during, "You guys are in for a real treat."

He knelt down, pulled the black bag from Parker Chandler's head.

Then he cursed.

Chandler's mouth was duct-taped, his eyes were shut, face sick-white.

Stanley said, "Is he dead?" breathing in through his nose, out through his mouth, trying not to vomit into his mask.

HS-3 said, "No, sir. We had to chloroform him pretty much every time he woke up because he wouldn't stop screaming."

Stanley covered his mouth with his hand.

He went upstairs.

Then up to the second floor bathroom.

He was on his knees in front of the toilet. Had to convince his guts that Chandler only looked dead, that Chandler being in the basement was no big deal, that the reasons for Stanley's bunker being chosen for this were because of his hard work, his incredible fan fiction, his hacks. That he deserved it.

He tried to keep quiet, puking.

But there was just so much.

• • •

Stanley wanted to recreate the scene from the novel where H-1 confronted the naïve narrator for the first time. Not the way it was in the movie, the movie was shit. But the way it was supposed to have been done.

But Chandler came to before Stanley finished gargling the taste of the stomach acid and lunch from the back of his throat.

Nervous, shaking, but empty, Stanley decided he should walk down the steps on the creakiest parts of the wooden planks. Slow. Deliberate. For effect. So Chandler would be fucking crying by the time he got down there.

But the stairs didn't groan. Not once.

Stanley, sweating under his mask, slumped his shoulders and took his seat in front of the man he'd once idolized.

Groggy, bleary-eyed, Chandler said, "Where am I?"

Deep breath. Then, "You are in a Hactivate bunker at a classified location."

"Holy shit, you can't be serious. You're not serious, are you?"

"Why wouldn't I be?"

"Because *Hactivate* was a novel, you moron. Fiction. It's all fake."

Stanley slapped Chandler across the face. Had to stop himself from shaking off the sting in his hand. "It's more than that and you know it."

"No, it's not. It's—"

"A manifesto disguised as a work of fiction to keep the idiotic powers-that-be at bay."

Chandler rolled his eyes, laughed, sat back in his chair.

Stanley said, "You were a hero, Parker. And you're going to throw it away."

"This is about *Hactivate 2*, then? Look, I know how real this feels. But I was just like you. This is all an act, man. I'm under contract so I can't say much more, but the stupid stunts Maxwell puts me up to haven't worked all that well lately, my sales have been tapering off a bit, so I wrote a sequel."

"That you decided to bastardize by injecting yourself into it? Metafiction blows, man."

"That's what *Hactivate* would be if I actually meant a word that was written in there, you nut."

Stanley heard his teeth grinding in his head. Felt the heat in his jaw.

Chandler said, "The book's not even that good. *Defamation by Proxy*, *A World Made Sallow*, and *Filmmaker, Filmmaker* are way better."

"Oh, come on. *Filmmaker, Filmmaker* sucks."

"It was my most honest work. Swear to God."

"We in Hactivate do not bow to false deities."

"Oh, for fuck's sake."

"You wrote that. Those are your words."

"I made them up. They don't mean anything. Wait, did Maxwell put you up to this? This is all just a joke, right? A publicity stunt? I've got to admit, it's a new one. Bold. But fucked up."

Stanley stood, said, "No, Parker. It's not a joke." He held out a hand, said, "H-111," closed his eyes, and concentrated on stopping his hand from shaking until he felt metal weigh down his palm.

Chandler said, "Holy fuck. Look, man. You can't do this. You've got the wrong fucking—"

Stanley said, "Shut up," pressed the gun barrel to Chandler's forehead. He said, "Your De-Education begins at oh-four-hundred hours."

H-111 cleared his throat, said, "That's four in the morning, sir."

"Oh-six-hundred hours." Stanley cocked the gun, said, "Now. Mr. Chandler. The Moto."

Sobbing, slobbering, Parker Chandler said the words he wrote two decades ago.

• • •

The De-Education of Parker Chandler came word for word from the novel. Duct-taped mouth, zip-tied hands, blacked eyes—every detail counted.

Stanley even had the honor of giving Chandler his new name. Void.

Stanley forced Void to watch the destruction of his former self.

A burn barrel was set up in the backyard. Void's driver's license, debit card, credit cards, social security card, everything in his wallet went in first. Then his clothes. Then it was clumps of his hair as Stanley sheered it off.

But the stink made Stanley hand over the rest of the initial duties to H-110.

Void was locked in one of the basement closets. The only thing Stanley left for him inside was an old boom box loaded with a cassette tape that played the Motto over and over again in various tones of voice. The volume was up so high it could be heard seeping up through the floorboards from the second story. Every forty minutes for twenty-four hours Stanley had Nothing or Nobody flip the tape over.

Stanley asked H-107 to do the honors of force-feeding Void wet Alpo for dinner on the third evening.

Gun in his shaky hand, barrel at Void's temple, Stanley said, "Why do we eat that which was meant for animals?"

Slurping, chomping, Void gagged through his response, "We are animals ourselves."

"How can we become more than animals?"

Void didn't make it through the next answer. Everything he swallowed was slopping down the front of him.

Stanley handed the gun over to 107, breathed deep, said, "Start again."

Then he went upstairs to lay down a while.

Despite his queasy stomach, he forced himself to settle his nerves. He had to do everything right. He was given this responsibility because of everything he'd done for Hactivate, because the right people had taken notice, because he was a valuable asset to the cause.

So he went back to work.

He gave Void the choice between washing out his honeybucket with his daily ration of water or having something to drink. Made him to watch the most violent films H-104 had in his DVD collection in lieu of the actual Desensitization Tapes that hadn't yet been delivered from Amazon. Had him sleep sitting up, made sure he was scared awake at random intervals.

On the fifth day, Stanley sent an H-Mail alerting H-0 that Void had given in, that he had nothing else to say but the Motto when the duct-tape was off. And would say it over and over and over.

Stanley was then ordered to Disseminate.

He used the Hactivate Server to reveal to the world that unless *Hactivate 2* was pulled from the presses, Parker Chandler would be dead before the first copy was sold.

Then he posted a pic of Void tied up in the basement so the idiotic powers-that-be would know that Stanley was not fucking around.

• • •

Void's Hactivation ceremony was held in the backyard.

In the center of the grass square, H-101 through H-114 stood in front of the tall bushes that lined the picket fence in their pressed Hactivate fatigues, polished boots, and balaclavas.

Stanley designated Numbers to Nobody and Nothing, asked them to pull their standard issue Hactivate pistol that had been tucked into the back of their pants.

Nobody opened his mouth, wrapped his lips around the barrel, pulled the trigger. With the click he was named H-115. Stanley said, "Nobody no more."

Nothing hesitated, took a breath, put the gun in his mouth and pulled the trigger. Another click. He was H-116. Stanley said, "Nothing no more."

Stanley stood in front of Void, pulled the duct tape from his cracked, bloody lips, asked if he was ready.

Sitting, tied to his chair, Void said, "Yes, sir."

Stanley waved, and H-109 untied Void.

Stanley told Void to stand.

Void said, "Yes, sir."

Face to face, Stanley and Void said the Motto together.

Then Void head-butted Stanley in the face.

The sound Stanley's nose made was worse than the pain. But the pain came in heavy waves. When it was most intense, Stanley started with the opening letter of a curse, then screamed the remaining syllable. When the pain ebbed a bit, he opened his eyes.

His men were chasing Void around the yard.

Void was screaming. "Where's the fucking door," and, "Someone fucking help me," and, "I'm not Parker fucking Chandler."

Stanley stood, ordered his men to make Void shut his mouth before the neighbors on the other side of the woods heard him.

Void screamed louder.

Stanley bled all over his hands, his fatigues.

He was gagging, watching as his men tackled Void and beat him into the grass.

• • •

The surgical tape holding the splint to Stanley's nose made him claw at his face. The itch wouldn't go away. He'd have to re-tape it after he dealt with Void.

Tied up and passed out, Void snored in his chloroformed sleep. Stanley sat in a wooden chair feet away.

He wasn't going to fuck this up. Couldn't fuck this up.

He snapped his fingers. He couldn't see H-115 and 116 moving, only heard them shuffling across the floor, grunting while carrying the bucket every Hactivate member was asked to piss into over the past couple hours.

Stanley had to keep telling himself it was just water, that's all, just water.

He took a breath, said, "Do it."

The new Hactivatists lifted the bucket over Void's head, drenched him in stinking liquid.

Void screamed himself awake.

Then he wept.

He must have remembered this scene from his novel. He said no, no, no over and over until Stanley told him to shut his mewling trap.

"Why are you doing this to me," Void said.

Stanley leaned back in his chair, crossed his arms. He waited for Void to stop crying.

Void spat on the floor, stared Stanley in the eye, said, "I'm going to fucking kill you. No, first I'll find your family and skin them alive. Then I'll cook them into a stew and force-feed them to you until you die from gorging yourself."

There was a gasp behind Stanley. Whether it was H-115 or 116 he couldn't tell. But it didn't matter. He clapped his hands, stood up, said, "That's the spirit, Void. That's the true Hactivate spirit running through you."

Void said, "There is no Hactivate spirit, you psycho. There's not even a Parker Chandler. Not for a long time. It's all bullshit." Then he spat into Stanley's face, sprayed snot and urine onto his lips.

Stanley leaned to the side, let go of his lunch all over the floor.

Then he asked for H-116's gun.

H-116 said, "But, sir—"

Hand out, Stanley said, "Shut it."

H-116's gun in his hand, he stood, kicked his seat over, and told Void to open his mouth.

"Fuck you. Let me go. I'm not Parker Chandler. Parker Chandler is dead."

Stanley said, "Not yet," and snapped his fingers.

H-115 and 116 moved behind Void, grabbed his head, pulled his mouth open.

There was a scream, a snap of bone, a spritz of blood.

H-116 fell to the floor screaming.

Void spit the first inch of a finger to the floor.

That's when Stanley stood up, cocked the pistol, and put a bullet through Void's eye.

Skull bits, globs of brain, and blood slapped against the wall.

Nothing happened for one, two, three seconds, until Stanley began screaming. High-pitched, shrill, and prolonged, he shrieked until he used up all the air in his lungs. Then swallowed a deep breath and started again.

Most of the Hactivatists were gone before Stanley stopped screaming.

H-116, writhing on the floor, said, "I didn't sign up for this bullshit."

Stanley grabbed H-116 by the front of his shirt, dragged him into a sitting position, said, "You loaded your fucking gun?"

"What else are you supposed to do with a gun?"

"You never read the fucking book, did you? That movie was shit."

"I tried to tell you the gun was—"

"Fuck you. That fucking movie was fuck—"

Stanley threw up what little was left in his stomach onto H-116's chest.

Together on the floor they listened to the sirens get louder and louder.

• • •

Stanley's trial was quick. Books were thrown. Kidnapping and murder were proverbial cherries on top of stacks of criminal charges that included—but were not limited to—the dissemination of multitudinous government secrets that lead to the losses of billions of dollars worldwide over the span of a decade.

But Stanley knew all that. It was his job.

He was called a monster by the media.

A traitor by the President.

A shitty writer by the internet—they'd found his fan fiction, made memes out of the stuff.

General population proved to be problematic.

Once the other inmates had discovered his squeamishness, Stanley was puking more than he was eating. And after his third hospitalization from dehydration and the beginnings of starvation, he was placed in solitary.

But even the guards were fucking with him.

He found the loogie before taking a bite of his meatloaf. The guard on duty had been suffering from a sinus infection.

Stanley gagged, placed his tray onto the cell floor, took a breath, said, "Very funny."

But no one was listening. His voice echoed down the concrete hall.

His stomach was shaky. His palms were sweaty. His lips glommed together with white goo. And he stared at his feet, counting his breaths, trying to hold onto his lunch—which was more than likely also soiled.

Then there were footsteps. Two sets.

They grew louder and louder until one stopped in front of his cell.

Someone said his name. His real name. H-100.

Stanley said, "Who are you?"

"I am H-0," a man said, stepping into view. "But you know my birth name, surely."

The last time Stanley had seen this man was on television just before the Philadelphia Riots. His birth name could be found on the acknowledgements page of every Parker Chandler novel. Cornelius Maxwell, literary agent.

Stanley said, "What are you doing here?"

"I'm here to get you out of this place."

"Who sent you?"

"I sent myself."

Stanley stood, wrapped his hands around the bars of his cell, said, "It was you." He pressed his forehead to the cool metal, said, "The whole time?"

Maxwell laughed, said, "Surprised you hadn't figured that out already. Regardless, Hactivate must always have a leader. You allegedly killed that leader."

"Parker Chandler was a charlatan. He was nothing. Said so himself."

Maxwell laughed, hard this time. "You don't know what you're a part of, do you?"

"I'm not a part of anything. This whole thing was nothing. Just a handful of hackers with no lives."

"Was Hemingway the one who came up with the iceberg thing? Doesn't matter." Maxwell snapped his fingers. Another man, the other set of footsteps, came forward.

Dylan didn't want to gasp—people only gasped in shit fiction—but he did it anyway.

The man standing to Maxwell's left was a perfect copy of Stanley.

Maxwell said, "This is H-10K986, surgically transformed and prepared to rot in a cell for the rest of his life for Hactivate."

Stanley said nothing.

There was a buzz, the sound of the cell door unlocking.

Maxwell pulled the door open, waved for Stanley to step outside.

H-10K986 took Stanley's place, recited the Motto, then said, "Thy will be done, sir."

Stanley followed Maxwell down the hall asking every question he could think of, spitting them in rapid succession.

Maxwell said, "Men on the inside," and, "You'll understand soon enough." Then he asked a question of his own, said, "Are you ready?"

"To get out of here? Fucking-A right, I am."

Laughing again, Maxwell said, "No, no. I mean, are you ready to become the new Parker Chandler?"

Stanley stopped, said what.

"I love your fan fiction, H-100. Our second iteration's work got all pretentious and weird. Who writes themselves in their own stories? Regardless, the world needs a proper Chandler."

"But he's dead."

"No, he's not. The man you killed kidnapped Chandler, paid a fortune for dozens of plastic surgeries, stole his identity, kept him locked up in his basement. Or, maybe Chandler's long-lost twin showed up to his house unannounced and was black-bagged instead of the actual Chandler."

"Are you fucking with me?"

"Come with me and whatever we want to be the truth becomes the official story. Now, I'll ask again. Are you ready?"

Stanley smiled, followed Maxwell down the hall, up several flights of stairs, onto the roof and into a waiting helicopter.

In his seat, buckled up, he was told about the medical procedures he would need to go through. The contract he would need to sign to keep his trap shut should one of Chandler's "stunts" become a major situation. Again.

And before Maxwell could get through discussing the ins and outs of the responsibilities of being Parker Chandler, Stanley said, "Was the second Chandler the one who wrote *Filmmaker, Filmmaker*?"

Maxwell, yelling over the sound of the starting propellers, said, "We like not to think about that piece of shit. Hopefully you've got some better ideas."

Stanley smiled, said, "Fucking-A right I do."

LIV

The blood on Lisa's hands was sticky by morning. Came off in clumps and strips the second and third time she washed her hands in the bathroom sink. She couldn't look in the mirror. Not after what she'd seen when she first woke up. She'd have to get her hands clean first, get the stinking meat out from under her fingernails before she moved to her face. She'd already been crying from what she assumed was happening to her. Calmed herself down by the plans she'd made for after she was finished. But the scalding hot water turning her clean skin red again brought the tears back.

She scrubbed, rinsed, pumped more soap into her cupped hand, scrubbed, rinsed, and did it all over. She washed and washed. Then she checked and rechecked every inch of skin from her fingertips to above her wrists to make sure she'd gotten it all off. And even then, she stared at the mess of clotted blood and balled up flesh stuck around the stopper instead of looking herself in the face. The crusty, maroon-stained clothes on the floor instead of forcing her eyes to look up into the glass.

She said okay, okay, okay. Told herself to look, that she has to look. That the sooner she was clean, the sooner she could get this all taken care of. That she'd track down the idiot from the bar she'd pretended to like and had taken home over the weekend.

She counted.

One.

Two.

Three.

Whatever she'd attacked and killed and eaten must have been big. There was too much blood on her nose, around her mouth, coated on her lips, caked in her teeth to be a rabbit. Or a squirrel.

Or a cat.

And if she saw any of her neighbors stapling missing dog flyers to telephone polls on her way to the doctor's office she told herself that she'd never pick up strange men in dive bars ever again.

She gagged, tasted whatever she'd eaten last night on the back of her tongue.

Then she got to work.

• • •

It wasn't a dog. Lisa was glad for that.

But while she was bagging up what was left of the deer in the backyard, she kept throwing up and hoping her landlady wasn't watching through the upstairs window. It wouldn't have been the first time Kathy had caught her getting sick outside, but this was different. The judgments here would be based on something else entirely. Full of all those nasty words she'd heard every now and again since she was a teenager.

The deer was mostly bones and fur and tendons, but the thought of eating the poor thing's guts, stomach, and heart while it watched and bleated kept bringing it all back up.

After, she pulled the other garbage bags that were filled with actual trash out of the bin and set them aside. It was ridiculous, but she mourned for the time when she'd thrown away regular shit for a moment. Yesterday. The day before. Last week, before that moron was careless and selfish enough to crud her up. Once this was taken care of she'd go back to tossing old takeout containers, colorful party decorations, empty bottles, and everything else like she'd always had. But now something as simple as cleaning her apartment would always stink of rotting deer and whatever lousy cologne Matt...Marty...Mike...What's-His-Face was wearing. She couldn't and wouldn't call what she'd done with the guy a mistake. But now everything would be tainted. And she hated it.

She dropped the bag into the bottom of the bin. Stuffed the rest of the trash on top. Took a deep breath to settle her stomach. And then she heard her name spoken as if it were a rhetorical question.

Kathy, with a garbage bag in her hand, stood feet away from Lisa. Her eyebrow was cocked. Her jaw was clenched. She said, "Don't forget there's a hose back there."

Lisa smiled, tried out a casual laugh to shift the feeling in the air. She was about to run a hand through her hair before she remembered her hands were filthy again. Even though she was careful cleaning up the deer, her whole body squirmed with the same feeling.

"Yeah," she said. "Sorry. I'll take care of it."

Kathy's face didn't change. "This one didn't try to take anything on his way out, did he?"

Lisa almost said no. She couldn't believe she almost said no. Instead, she balled her fists. Felt her fingernails lengthening, sharpening, digging into her palms. "It'll be cleaned up before I leave."

"If I had known what I'd be getting into before having you sign the lease," Kathy said, "we certainly wouldn't be having this conversation."

Lisa ran her tongue along her sharpening canines. Felt the sting of their edges.

Then she smiled at Kathy.

The older woman's eyes widened. She took a step back.

And after Lisa clacked her jagged, knife-sharp jaws together three or four times, she said, "Have a nice day, Kathy." Then she brushed against her landlady as she passed her.

• • •

The doctor called in a prescription for Lisa. She imagined what the pharmacist on the other line was thinking. Something about how careless she was. How pathetic her life must've been to have gotten into this situation. How stupid she was to put herself and everyone around her in such danger.

It took nothing less than the doctor hanging up the phone and turning around to keep her from crying. With his back turned, she would've let everything building inside her go. But his facing her, smiling, explaining he was going to give her a tutorial held it all back.

His pen in his hand, the doctor said, "Okay. So, what you'll do is use it the same way someone with a severe allergy would use an EpiPen." He mimed injecting the point of the Bic into his thigh. "You've got to jab it in there pretty hard, okay? Once you do, hit the button on the top." He clicks the pen, leaves a black mark on his lab coat. "And that's that."

Lisa nodded, said, okay, okay. "And this has to be during the full moon?"

"Just before you feel yourself shifting, yes. If you shift, well, you won't be contagious anymore, but you know what'll happen."

Lisa remembered not remembering what she'd done last night. Waking up from a dreamless sleep. Then smelling the blood. Doing that once a month forever.

"Any questions?" the doctor said.

Lisa opened her mouth.

She couldn't speak.

"It's okay," the doctor said. "LIV isn't as rare as people think it is. It's still around and it affects hundreds of thousands of people a year. But there's nothing to be embarrassed about. You're getting it taken care of. You're—"

"I'm not embarrassed," Lisa said. "It's something else."

"What is it then?" the doctor said, folding his arms in front of him.

She didn't say anything. Couldn't say that there's something different now. Something she didn't know was there before but was gone. "Can I...give this to someone any other way?" she said, changing the subject.

"No," the doctor said. "This can only be transmitted one way. Old stories, the internet, legends, most of what you'll read about it is as false as the reports that say it's been virtually eradicated. You can't pass it along by biting or scratching someone, or forcing them to drink rainwater out of your footprint in the mud."

For a moment, Lisa wanted to rip the doctor's throat out with her teeth. Pull open his ribcage and eat his lungs. But then her stomach rolled over on itself. She said, "Okay."

"Keep your stress low. Stay calm. Yoga classes help for some people."

Lisa, fiddling with her paper gown said, "What happens if I get angry? Earlier today I—"

"You just want to keep yourself from shifting. Do that and this will all be over soon. Sound good?"

Lisa nodded.

The doctor said good, smiled, told her to have a nice day, and left the room.

And Lisa sat alone mostly naked for a while staring at the floor until the nurse came in and told her they'll need the room for the next patient.

• • •

When Lisa was a teenager, she'd drive her parents' car around a circuit of her favorite places. The mall. The movie theater. The diner. The convenience store. During the week since the deer, she'd visited all of those places. It's not as if she hadn't been there in fifteen years. She'd never stopped going to these places. But as she walked the mall, all the stores she used to shop in had disappeared and been replaced. She'd noticed before. But standing in a sporting goods store that now was in the spot where she bought most of her high school dance dresses felt like standing in a morgue.

She laughed at how melodramatic that thought was. Said to herself that she's now more American than ever before, mourning a store.

But here, right here, she picked a purple and pink floral print dress off the rack that made her feel good about herself when she tried it on. Made her feel healthy instead of skinny. Complimented her golden hair in contrast to the darkest purples in the fabric. Sometime since she'd forgotten how she felt in this spot, the dresses were replaced with a stack of boxed footballs.

This Distance

Across the store, there used to be plastic spinning racks with fake but high school-beautiful jewelry. She'd given her boyfriend hints and hints about a necklace she'd wanted for her birthday. He smiled at her, said okay, okay. And when her eighteenth birthday had come around, she unwrapped a box he'd handed her and pulled out that necklace. He'd told her he ran back into the store for it while she went to the bathroom with her friends. Whether or not it was true it didn't matter. She loved him for it and loved the necklace. And even though she can't remember what she'd done with it, she could almost feel the small amount of weight around her neck. The little chill of the pendant on her chest. The display was still a spinner rack. But now Fitbits were locked inside.

Lisa walked the store longer than she'd expected to. Hit every display, clothing rack, and corner in the store. She barely heard the kid ask her if she needed any help.

"No," she said. "I'm just looking."

"For anything in particular?" he said, scratching the side of his pimpled forehead.

"This used to be my favorite store."

"I'm into sports too."

"It was something else," Lisa said, regretting how fast she responded. She smiled, said, "I loved the dresses. It used to smell different in here too. Like all sorts of perfume all at once. It was nice. Now it smells like sneakers and balls."

The kid laughed.

"That's...that's not what I meant." Lisa felt her face heat up with the blood racing to the surface. Felt like everyone in the store had heard her, heard the kid laughing at her. The only thing she'd wanted to do was to sleep, eat, go to work, repeat until the full moon. To stick to the margins until she was healthy again. But now it was almost as if everyone in the store knew that she was a walking infection. That she could turn into a monster any second.

The kid told her to let him know if she needed anything, and walked back to the register. And ten, fifteen feet away, she could smell his deodorant. His second-wear socks. His acne medicine. The puss in his zits.

Her own blood.

Lisa had dug bloody crescent moons into her palms. Could smell everything on everyone in the store. Could hear the end of each breath rumble into a growl.

To calm herself, she walked back to the stack of footballs. And one by one, she pierced each ball with a clawed finger.

· · ·

Rolling up her yoga mat, Annie asked Lisa how she felt about the class.

"A little sore," Lisa said.

Annie laughed, said seriously.

"For most of the last hour I felt pretty good."

"Good. See? You just needed to get your mind—"

"Until the instructor told us to get into the Downward Dog position." Lisa unrolled her mat, pointed to the claw marks.

"I can lend you my spare for next time," Annie said.

Over lunch, Annie talked about her job. How she was thinking about starting to save for a house. How Rob was definitely going to propose, he was just dragging his feet a little. How she would like to start having kids as soon as they were married, might even quit her birth control the month before the wedding—whenever that happened to be.

And Lisa was happy for her friend. Since high school she'd always been just a step behind Annie though. Grades, college acceptances, jobs, boyfriends. But no matter where Lisa was in her own life, whenever Annie was succeeding—which was pretty much all the time—she felt good about all of it.

But whenever there was a lull in the conversation, Annie even took a bite of her sandwich or a sip of her bright pink smoothie, Lisa's brain went right back to her LIV. To her normally more-than-healthy sexual appetite being nonexistent. To her dinners since the doctor's appointment consisting of rarer and rarer burger until a week ago when she ate the raw chuck right out of the Styrofoam and shrink wrap. To the urge to track down Mitch...Marvin...Mario...whatever, and disembowel him while he screamed for help that wouldn't come. After those thoughts started she bought herself spirals of sausage from the supermarket and ate them in her car.

Lisa heard her name.

Annie was tapping her bottom lip, her eyes wide.

Only then did Lisa taste the blood. She'd fanged out, shredded the inside of her mouth.

She pulled her phone from her pocket, turned the camera to face her, said shit.

Red lipstick never worked for her before and it didn't work then.

"It's almost over," Annie said.

Lisa laughed a little, her eyes welled up a bit. She said, "No it's not."

Annie passed her a napkin, said, "Of course it is. The full moon's just—"

"That won't be enough," Lisa said, dabbing her lips, leaving clumps of paper stuck around her mouth.

"What do you mean?"

Lisa popped her claws, said, "This is what I mean."

Annie looked around the restaurant. And Lisa watched her eyes go from table to table. "It doesn't matter if they look."

She let the rest of the non-full moon transformation wash over her. Felt her forehead angle itself into angry ridges, hair sprout from her cheeks forming raggedy muttonchops, watched her vision switch from full color to grays and blacks and whites and reds where she could see people's body heat radiating from them.

Now people were staring.

Her fangs gave her a lisp, but she talked anyway, a growl rounding off the end of her sentences. "I won't look like this after the injection. But I'll still be this. And I'll feel like I feel now all the time."

Lisa shifted herself back to normal. Which was a word that felt more like a curse than anything else.

Annie didn't say anything. Just had that look on her face she'd had every time Lisa had failed at something, whatever it was. Halfway between pity and sympathy.

Lisa picked the rest of the napkin from her lips as some people at the surrounding tables started gathering their things to leave.

"Oh, stop," Lisa said. "You'd have to fuck me to get what I've got. And we all know no one wants that."

Lisa and Annie ate their lunch in silence for a while before Lisa apologized. Before she figured she had nothing to apologize for anyway. Before she didn't really care what Annie thought right then.

. . .

Every night of the week before the full moon, Lisa had gone back to the bar where she met Manny...Mark...Melvin...whatever. She sat and drank beer and ate burgers and chicken tenders and roast beef sandwiches. Played darts alone. Played pool with an old drunk who kept calling her cutie and sweetie and hun. Did shots for last call with whoever wanted one—she was always buying. And the guy didn't show up night after night.

Lisa couldn't figure out what she'd say to him if he were to show up. She knew what she wanted to do but knew she couldn't do. But she waited for him anyway. No one would go to this dump if it weren't a place they'd been going for years. So far she'd been wrong, but it was a solid hypothesis. Between the stale beer stink, the middle-aged guys who would show up every night, and the bartender who only typically charged for the first beer, it was a good bet.

She'd only come in here in the first place because she wanted to get drunk and laid and it was the closest place to her office.

So maybe she was wrong.

If she did it, what's to say the guy didn't do the same thing.

Friday night, Lisa took a sip of beer, checked the time on her phone. Bit into a barely cooked burger, looked at the clock hanging over the liquor bottles. Collected her winnings from the drunken pool player, asked him what time it was.

She still had time.

Not much.

But still.

It was a quarter past eleven when she thought she'd better head home. She needed her injection soon. Twelve-oh-seven, twelve-oh-seven, twelve-oh-seven, she repeated it in her head like a mantra. Say something enough and its meaning will melt into phonemes, and for once since everything happened, Lisa didn't feel like people could see the infection crawling around under her skin. And for a moment, she was calm.

That's when he walked in.

He fist-bumped the drunk, said yo to the bartender, and sat three stools down from Lisa. Didn't even see her.

Lisa drained her beer, turned, said, "Hey, you," all flirty. Just like last time.

Myron, Maynard, Marcus' eyes went wide. His skin drained of its color. Lisa could hear his heartbeat pick up its pace. "Hey. Hi. How are you?"

Lisa got up walked over to him, said, "I'm great now, Mike. How—"

"Brian."

"That's right. I'm great now, Brian. How are you?"

As they spoke, flirted, whatever, Lisa could smell the nervous sweat soaking into his shirt under his arms. Hear a droplet run from his back into his ass crack. Felt his irregular breathing on her face.

One look at the clock behind the bar and Lisa realized they'd talked a little too long.

She said, "Do you want to come back to my apartment, Brian?"

• • •

Lisa and Brian made too much noise getting through the door. Kathy was banging on the ceiling from upstairs before they made it to the bedroom.

Lisa pulled off Brian's shirt, unbuckled his belt, unzipped his pants, bit his bottom lip hard enough to draw blood.

"Ouch," he said. "Careful."

That's when Lisa shoved his near-naked ass onto her bed. "Careful?" she said, her voice shifting low and guttural.

Brian cursed.

More knocking from upstairs.

Her fangs fully formed, she said, "You're stupid enough to think I didn't get sick? Stupid enough to think that you got lucky not spreading your shit?" She was on top of him, her claws at his throat.

"I—I'm sorry. I'm so sorry."

"You're not sorry. Not really."

"I am. I didn't know."

Lisa laughed, hard.

Knocking from upstairs.

Eyes glowing, mouth watering and dripping in shimmering ropes onto Brian, Lisa said, "The symptoms are pretty fucking specific."

Brian was crying. Saying sorry over and over.

"You took something from me, Brian," Lisa said, her voice little more than an animal's growl.

"I didn't want to be alone," Brian said through his tears. "I wanted to forget about feeling like a freak."

"You're not anymore though, are you? I'm the only freak here, right?" Lisa could almost see the pale gold reflection of her eyes off Brian's oily skin.

He nodded.

Muffled, from upstairs, Kathy's voice came through the ceiling telling them to shut up or get out.

That's when Lisa stood and howled. Or roared. Or whatever the horrible, monstrous sound that came out of her chest could be called.

The knocking stopped.

Brian sucked back his apologies.

And Lisa felt something other than alone, or diseased, or sick. And it was good.

Her phone vibrated in her pocket.

Twelve-oh-seven.

Twelve-oh-seven.

Twelve-oh-seven.

Hairy, snarling, and starving, Lisa didn't move. Just stood there. The injector in the bathroom. Brian on the bed. Kathy upstairs. She stood there knowing there was nothing she could do to change anything.

Brain said something about needing to inject herself.

She told him to shut up.

He did.

And there was that feeling again.

Brain said, "What? What are you staring at?"

Lisa smiled. Showed her fangs.

Then Brian pissed himself and started screaming.

. . .

Lisa was outside.

It was morning.

The blood on her hands, under her fingernails, had dried into clumps.

She didn't have to hope that it wasn't a dog—it wasn't a dog.

Almost like she knew that she'd figured out when to stop. Like she hadn't completely lost herself. Like she was Lisa enough, even fully shifted, to remember where the line was.

She'd have to clean up what was left of the raccoon. Stuff it in the garbage again. Shower. Get to yoga with Annie. Maybe start looking for a new apartment.

Everything was different. She still wasn't the old her. She wasn't going to be that again no matter what she'd done. But she also wasn't a monster. Not a monster-monster at least.

She was new.

Not baby-new. Or innocent-new.

But she was something else now. And she didn't hate it.

Beginning Again, Or How to Murder Your Monster and Get Away with It

Your monster leaves green, wiry fur everywhere. He slops greasy white drool onto the furniture when he eats. His horns have splintered the door jambs and frames in nearly every room in the house. He never wipes his hooves before coming inside. He's got a wet dog smell when he's dry. A dead dog smell when he's wet. He never cleans up after himself. Cigarette butts. Beer bottles. Take out containers. Condom wrappers. All over the place. All the time. He steals cash right out of your wallet too.

And every time you've tried to murder him he's never, ever died. Not even once. Not even for a second.

But you keep trying.

You keep trying because if he's still mucking around, you're still making excuses. For the late nights. The inability to commit. The endless string of angry friends—former friends. For everything.

You cook up a beautiful breakfast of eggs and toast and waffles and bacon and sausage. You pepper it all with arsenic.

Your monster, he doesn't bother to thank you—because, of course, he doesn't—before he starts throwing clumps of food into his face.

But you don't care.

Not about the bits of egg that end up on the wall behind him. Not about the slurping, sucking sounds he makes while he chews. And not about the scratches he leaves in your good plates and custom, authentic Amish-crafted table, grabbing for more. (You bought that thing to show your mother, your father, your friends that you can take care of nice things. And now it's wrecked.)

So you laugh when he keels over, shatters a plate with his face.

The impact jingles the unused utensils. Spills juice and coffee over the rims of glasses and mugs.

His face in a bed of shattered ceramic, you're a cackling fiend. Your stomach muscles ache, you can't catch your breath, your eyes are all runny. A rope of slobber runs from your bottom lip to your tie.

All because now, starting today, you'll be taken seriously.

At work, you're a new man. Everyone sees it. Your boss. Lola from accounting. Your marketing team.

You've hit reset. You've got a chance to begin again. Like the song you used to sing as a kid—the one about the pathetic old Irish man.

Lola says, "You look happy today."

"Michael Finnegan begin again," you say. "What would you say to drinks? Monsterless. Just you and me?"

But, of course, your monster calls the office just after lunch to tell you how delicious breakfast was. To ask what you did differently.

A Google search later you find out that arsenic acts as a strong sedative for monsters. That it adds volume and body to their fur on top of the very deep, euphoric sleep it induces.

You cancel on Lola before you leave for the night.

• • •

The next time you give it a go, you get your monster good and drunk at the bar you two used to close-up almost nightly. Now just semi-nightly.

You act like he's your best buddy.

It's easy because he used to be.

You buy him beers, shots, mixed drinks. More beers, more shots, and even more shots. And you, you're faking sloppy while matching drink for drink. With a little help from the bartender, the beers are Becks NA in pint glasses. The white liquor is water. The brown liquor is...okay, it's brown liquor. But you don't blame yourself for that. You'll need the guts to do what needs to get done.

Your monster, he's cutting it up with other's people's monsters—the ones who have it together. The ones with their fur trimmed, and their horns polished, and their tusks or teeth all pearly white. Sure, they're playing pool and swearing and smoking and talking bawdy about the purple-furred, fanged waitress's scaly, sparkly tail...but most certainly they'll go home with their humans to get enough sleep so that they'll be ready for work bright and early.

The guys sitting at the bar with you, they're adults. They've tamed their monsters. Landed good jobs. Bought houses. And only get drunk and rowdy when their schedule permits.

Buy you, you've had enough of all of it. Enough for two monsters, really. And despite your monster refusing to cut it out with the drinking, the smoking, the everything, you're doing everything you can to separate yourself from that.

You talk to the bartender politely—because that's what you do now. Ask her what she does outside of this place, what her hobbies are, where she's from. You're friendly with the waitress-monster, who, like most, grew up properly alongside her human counterpart.

But that's when your monster loses everything he drank all over the pool table.

"He's yours, right?" the bartender says.

You smile, say, "Yeah. But our priorities are different these days."

You manage to get him into your car, buckle him in.

Then you remember the plan and unbuckle the belt as if it had buckled itself without your permission.

It's dark. Dark-dark. No stars-dark. Just the halos from your headlamps crammed into yellow binoculars on the road. A streetlamp once or twice. Headlights every now and then. A police cruiser tucked behind some bushes here or there.

Before, this stretch of road at this time of night was just about the loneliest you could get.

Tonight—your monster snoring and slobbering all over himself in the passenger seat—you could scare children to tears with the grin stretching your face achy.

The bolt cutters bite through the chain at the quarry entrance with almost no effort. Maybe it's the adrenaline. Maybe the lightweight lifting is paying off. Maybe it was a bad chain because what kind of lunatic breaks into a quarry in the middle of the night?

Headlights off, the gravel's a whispering rumble under the tires.

Your monster doesn't stir, move, adjust. Doesn't make a sound. Not a grunt. Not a deep, wet, drunken burp. Nothing.

But a hundred or so feet from the hole, you're giggling.

The football helmet from high school smells too much like the past you hated while you lived it for no other reason than you were young and stupid and lonely. But it's nice now. Like the prom, you shouldn't have drunk through. The graduation you should've paid attention to. The couple of friends you should've kept in touch with.

One more big old whiff of sweat and dry rot, and you slam your foot onto the gas pedal, throw the car into drive, and take off toward the drop edge of nothing.

Just before the car sails into the black, you open the door and dive into the gravel. The momentum drags you through the dirt. Eats at your knees, hands, elbows, chest. But you don't care. There's plenty of time left to stop yourself before you roll over the edge.

Now that he's gone.

The Uber ride home is silent. Every now and again you hum about the Irish guy in that kiddie song. Every so often your brain replays the sound of the car hitting the bottom of the pit. And every time crumpling metal smashing against stone fires through your head, you add to a list of ways your life is about to improve.

Promotion: Possible.

Lose thirty pounds of fat, gain fifteen of muscle: In-Progress.

Lola falling in love with you: Be your new self and make it happen.

At home, in bed, sleep doesn't come easy because of the wonderful potential future ahead. But you drift off. Nice and slow, you drift away to be replaced by a brand new you in the morning.

• • •

Your monster calls from the police station first thing.

You have to burn some PTO to pick him up. Have to empty out your savings for bail.

At the station, your dinged up, bandaged, bruised monster acts all sheepish behind bars. He smiles, waves.

"He's yours, right?" an officer says.

You say nothing. Nod.

Once he's let out of his cell, you throw your arms around your monster, hug him tight. Then you say thank god, that you were worried sick, that you wouldn't know what you'd do without him.

The cop says your monster was lucky. But not lucky enough to walk away from an accident like that without any consequences. There will be a hearing. Probably required community service. Restitution. Maybe thirty days in jail depending on how the lenient the judge is with first-time monster offenders.

You're also told you need to be more responsible. "He is yours after all. Lead by example."

You hug your monster again, a bit tighter this time.

Face in his reeking green fur, you listen for a pained grunt or a slight crackle of bone. But he doesn't make a sound.

• • •

It's weeks before you even begin to think about trying again.

Longer until you wonder if you're the one who has to get murdered in order to get rid of your monster. But dying wouldn't work at all. That productive-member-of-society status you want so badly wouldn't apply to you. Lola from accounting would forget all about you, start talking to Dan from marketing, or Brian from the leadership team, or Ken from HR before too long. And your debt would get shunted back onto your sad, disappointed parents.

But when your monster falls asleep on the couch after talking about how wild that purple-furred, fanged waitress is, you turn all the gas burners on in the kitchen.

While gas stink fills the house, you're on your computer.

You google, are monsters flame retardant? How many monsters died in fires in the last ten years? Does monster fur gain a new lustrous color after being burned?

You google, will Lola forgive you for canceling on her so many times if personal tragedy strikes? How much time off will you get for being caught in a catastrophe? Is a person whole if their monster dies?

You're lightheaded when you reach for the scented candle on the coffee table. The scented candle you bought when your friends started putting scented candles on display in their lovely, well-maintained homes.

You pull the lighter that's tucked between cigarettes in your monster's pack of smokes. And when you flick the flame on, light the wick, you spring off the couch toward the door.

The explosion throws you through the screen door, down the porch steps, and spills you onto the little patch of lawn the landlord mows.

Aching, burned, bleeding, you laugh and laugh. You spit blood and laugh and laugh. And you have to force yourself to stop when the fire trucks and cops and ambulances show up, turn the neighborhood into a rave with their lights.

You answer all their questions lying on a stretcher.

"My monster was in there."

"I smelled gas right before it happened."

"I lit a candle. Is this my fault?"

The looks you get. Halfway between pity and scorn.

The same looks you've been getting since you and your monster never stopped yourselves from acting like you acted in high school. And college. And young-professionaldom. And middle-agedness. A boy and his monster, all grown up never having grown the fuck up.

"I'm alive now," you say. "I'm alive."

One of the paramedics, she turns to you, sort of smiles. "You're very lucky."

You laugh again.

That song floods your brain. The one about the Irish guy who never did anything right but always got second chances. The one you sang when you were a kid. Before you and your monster turned yourselves into beasts together.

Through your mangled, bloody smile, you say, "Luck had nothing to do with it. Poor old Michael Finnegan, begin again."

Then you start to sing. "Poor old Michael Finnegan, begin again."

Just before the EMTs shut the ambulance doors, someone outside says something like wait, wait, look. Something that sounds a lot like they've found something under whatever's left of your apartment.

That something's alive under there.

So you sing all the way to the hospital. You sing because you're going to get another shot. Whatever it is, you'll get another go at it.

Again and again.

Until it's right.

Hero Complex

Kelly doesn't remember me. She can't. When she woke up she couldn't remember anything. Couldn't speak.

But she was able to write. I saw the notes she would scribble.

Who was I? Why I was there, spending so much time in her hospital room. Always the same questions. Every night. Notes handed off to her parents about me.

Her parents would ask me the same questions. Only they knew exactly who I was, knew what I did.

Now, through the skylight, I watch her mother bring her a bowl of soup and a sandwich with the crust cut off. Kelly smiles at her mother, thanks her the best she can now that she's started talking a bit.

I buckle my helmet in place, take another look at her.

She doesn't remember.

But I do.

• • •

The *Daily News* sitting in the rack at the corner store has a grainy photo of the Night on the front page. From a traffic camera, probably. The headline's expected, nasty, accusatory.

I wince, clench my jaw, stretch to reach a copy near the bottom of the stand.

They attempt to hide the column regarding their increased readership at the bottom of the front page like it's an afterthought. It doesn't discuss the corollary between the Night showing up and the paper's selling copies as collector's items when they actually snap a photo of him and print it on the front page. It's just a nice, ancillary puff piece stuffed underneath a story about the city's first vigilante—superhero, whatever.

The clerk asks me if I'm going to buy the paper or what.

I apologize, smile, limp to the counter.

"You alright, pal?" he says.

I say, "Absolutely," smile again.

He stares at my mouth. He asks me to smile again.

Then I notice the taste. The metal. I feel my lips sticking together.

"Bit my tongue," I say.

"Off?"

I laugh, say, "Almost."

"Jesus."

Placing the paper down on the counter, I ask for a napkin.

He hands me one, and I'm careful to make sure paper fibers don't ball up, flake off and stick to my lips as I wipe the blood away from the corners of my mouth, my teeth.

"Paper's a buck," he says.

"Oh, can I have a coffee, too, please?"

"Won't that hurt?" he says, his voice cracking a bit, jumpy from the bleeding nutcase in his store.

I smile again, hoping I've wiped the blood away enough to make it more pleasant to look at, say, "I sort of got used to the pain."

• • •

At my arbitration hearing, a room full of people in suits thanks me for coming. They tell me to take a seat, and I try not to smile as I shake their hands. They're cordial, nodding their heads as I go down the line. They look at my hand, bandaged and seeping, but I tell them it's a pleasure to meet them so their gaze doesn't linger. But even then I'm sure they notice the swelling around my eye.

My principal, at the end of the line, doesn't shake my hand. Her eyes go to my mouth.

I wipe my lips with a tissue. There's still some blood, but not much.

My union rep tells me to let her do most of the talking. With her hand on my back, she turns me to where I'm supposed to sit.

I say, "Okay." I say, "How's it looking?"

She doesn't say anything, purses her lips, motions for me to sit down.

I sit, feel my knee pop, lock into a half-bent wreck. The pain pulses in the corners of my eyes, leaving spots in my periphery.

The people who were so nice when I entered the room are now speaking in stern tones about the position I've put myself in over the last several months. They talk about what my students have said about me. They talk about what my principal has reported. My running out of sick time but calling out anyway. My black eyes, my limping, my broken fingers.

They speak, but I only hear buzzwords as I work on my knee, massaging the kneecap, trying to straighten the leg.

I hear Suspension.

Hear, Responsibility.

Hear, Egregious lack of…something.

My union rep says, "What a teacher does outside of work is his or her own business."

Someone at the table says, "But when that affects the students' progress in the classroom that's when we have to look more closely at what one of our teachers does off-hours."

The table and my rep begin to get heated, discussing my case as if I'm not in the room.

My forehead, now slick with a sheen of sweat, begins to ache from all of the grimacing. The heat in my mouth from my split tongue is met, increased by my grinding teeth, which singe the inside of my cheeks.

I hear someone ask me if I'm listening, tell me how serious this is.

Smiling with my lips clamped shut I tell them, yes, I'm listening.

"What's the matter?" my union rep says, whispering in my ear.

"Nothing," I say.

"They won't terminate you today," she says.

"Good."

"They'll wait for the next hearing to do that."

Someone at the table clears their throat, begins speaking.

I push my kneecap to the right, to the left. I feel tendons, ligaments grating against bone while the man behind the table speaks to me in a calm, firm tone.

My knee pops, echoes through the room. I release a long, loud breath, smile as I stretch my leg.

I hear someone say, suspended without pay.

I say, "I'm sorry, what?"

· · ·

Kelly answers the door, her right arm locked into a crutch, her face confused and frightened that her mother wasn't the one who rang the doorbell. She doesn't recognize me, but when her eyes fall to the bouquet of flowers her mouth hooks into a half smile.

I ask her if she remembers me, hoping that after this long something may have come back to her.

"No," she says, her mouth working slow, deliberate. "Wait, you came to visit me in the hospital, right?"

I smile, tell her yes I did, tell her that we used to be friends. Years ago. I ask if she has gotten the flowers I've been sending her.

"No," she says. "I don't think so."

"Well, I brought you some more. You can have them if you want them."

"They're pretty," she says.

"Your favorite."

I turn and look back to the driveway, say, "Can I come in? Put them in water for you?"

"I don't know," she says. "My Mom told me when I was a kid I shouldn't let strangers in. With my memory the way it is she still tells me that."

"But I'm not a stranger, remember?"

She stares at me, her eyes dart from my face to the flowers. She doesn't fully recognize what it is, but there's something in there deep, making her hesitate, making her think that I'm okay, that I'm a good guy.

I hold the flowers to her, place my hand on the screen door so she can take them. "What do you think?" I say. "I'm a friend, I swear."

She nods, turns and moves toward the kitchen without taking the flowers from me.

Glancing back at the driveway before I enter, I step into the house. I haven't set foot in here since just after college. When we were still together. I remember her then. Fit and firm, she filled out her clothes with a body that I couldn't help but stare at. But now as she hobbles through the foyer I see up close how much of that person has faded away. Her pants are loose, her shirt hangs from her shoulders.

Her smile's gone.

I go to the sink, take a tall glass from the cabinet, fill it with water. Unwrapping her flowers, dropping them into the glass, I try to arrange them the best I can. But my hands are shaking too much.

I turn, try to tell her how much she loves these flowers. But I stop when I see her. Facing me, shoulders slouched, eyebrows bent toward the space between her eyes, she stands there. Staring at me.

She says, "You."

I say her name, take a step forward.

"No," she says.

"No? No, what? What's the matter?"

"You."

"Do—do you remember me?"

"You did this to me."

I take another step. She flinches.

I say, "No. I—"

I can't finish my sentence. A car honks in the driveway.

Her mother must already be out of the car.

Kelly lunges at me but catches her crutch on a chair at the kitchen table. Her face shifts from anger to horror as she loses her balance, collapses to the floor. Her knee hits first, then her shoulder. The sound of her face colliding with the floor makes me drop the flowers. The glass shatters, water bursts up and sloshes on her, soaking her.

The door clicks, unlocks. But before it opens I'm stepping over Kelly, running through the living room to the French doors that lead to the backyard.

Outside I sprint away, hearing the screams fade behind me.

• • •

I hold the lighter to the hooked needle until my fingers burn, pinching the metal at its base.

Taking the entire glass of whiskey down, I wait for the needle to cool.

I pinch the torn flesh together just under my nipple, weave the needle through in tight loops, drawing the hypoallergenic thread through fast enough that I don't forget how much this actually hurts before I run it through my skin again.

My breathing becomes a series of short inhalations. The volume of each breath increases every time I push the needle in, poke it through the other side.

Learning to sew stitches from instructional YouTube videos makes for ugly, jagged scars, but running to the hospital every time I get shanked in an alley, or slashed in a brawl isn't in my best interest.

I snip the thread close enough to feel the scissors graze my swollen skin, and pour peroxide over the closed wound. It barely stings at all. The whiskey's kicking in too late. I can never gauge how long to wait between chugging booze and stitching myself up. This one bled so much I think I made the right choice, though.

Leaving the bathroom, careful not to forget the bottle on the sink, I notice all the blood on the bedroom carpet and take note that I'll need to shampoo the stains out when I wake up tomorrow—actually, later today. It must have gushed onto the Berber after I unzipped the Kevlar tunic without my noticing. Sloppy.

I drop onto the couch and can't help but remember the sound Kelly's face made on the kitchen floor. I heard that sound while punching in the teeth of the guy who stabbed me. Heard it sound when my bloody vest smacked onto the tile floor in the bathroom. It's the only sound I hear over the ringing in my ears and the reruns on television.

I take another pull from the bottle, now just a slow, dull burn.

Putting my feet up on the coffee table I kick the remote to the floor. The plastic slapping onto the hardwood is Kelly's face again.

Now, with nowhere to go in the morning, I finish off the whiskey and drop the empty bottle onto the couch hoping not to hear that sound again.

• • •

We fought. All the time.

It was our thing. We would fight. Fuck. Wake up the next day and do the same thing all over again. It was our process. Never mind what friends and family would say about the emotional abuse. Those bruises we could hide easy enough.

The others, when she would bite me too hard, or I would hold onto her hips with a bit too much pressure, those are the ones we loved. The ones we couldn't get enough of. We would scar each other and laugh, and the laughing would turn to touching, and the touching would start the whole process over again.

Oddly happy, and happily miserable. That was us.

With love like that, though, everyone eventually crosses a line.

I talked to Jackie too long one night at a party. Or maybe I stared at Cora's ass over Kelly's shoulder when she was telling me to stop talking to Erica. I can't remember. It turned into a blend of jealousy and rage that threw Kelly over the top. She slapped me in front of everyone there.

I grabbed her arm and we left, screaming at each other down the street.

She threw me against the car, mashed her lips into mine after I told her I was fucking sorry. My lip bled, dripped onto her chin. She told me I was in some serious trouble and I should get us back to her house as soon as I could. Otherwise, she might've cooled off. And I wouldn't have wanted that.

Driving home she started talking about how bad she wanted to climb on top of Jackie's boyfriend.

I just drove, gripping the steering wheel harder and harder until my hands cramped up. I knew what she was doing. I knew she would resort to that tactic to get me more jealous than she was. But I didn't say anything.

Until she told me she thinks about him when we're fucking.

I lost it. I screamed at her. Used words I only used when she told me to.

We were on Broad Street when I pulled over and told her to get out of the fucking car.

She laughed, but I said, "Stop fucking laughing. Get out."

When she started crying I got out and walked around to her side. I opened the door, pulled her out.

She told me if I left her we were done.

I got in the car and drove away.

I turned my phone off. I screamed lines I wished I'd said while she was still there, had a conversation with myself almost all the way to her place. I wish I could say that I turned back around because I felt awful for leaving her.

I just didn't have a key to her place.

I called her to ask her where she was, but her phone rattled around the cup holder where she left it. She didn't have time enough to grab it before I ripped her out of the car.

It didn't take long to find her.

There was an ambulance, red, white, and blue lights a couple blocks down, around the corner from where I dropped her off.

I didn't bother to find a spot. I threw the car in park, got out and ran. There were cops everywhere.

She was lying on a gurney, her head strapped into an orange brace, her face covered in blood from where her eye socket was smashed in, where her head was cracked open. Her clothes were torn up, covered in blood.

They loaded her into the ambulance, holding a mask over her face, pumping oxygen into her mouth. I was screaming for someone to tell me what happened. I screamed until the cops asked me who I was, why I was there, who was I to her.

And I told them.

I told them everything that wouldn't make them believe I was responsible.

• • •

Running the shampooer over the carpet I realize I waited too long. The blood caked into scabs of polypropylene, hardened brown lily pads of varying sizes and shapes.

I hear the knock at my door over the machine. I shut the thing off and listen. I'm quiet, still, hoping whoever is there will get lost so I can finish up before suiting up and heading out for the night.

But they knock again.

I close my bedroom door, locking the bloody mess away. "Just a minute," I say, kicking a steel-toed boot into the closet and shutting it.

It's a cop.

I ask him how I can help him.

He asks if I am the name he reads from the paper he's holding.

"That's me," I say.

"You've been served, sir. You'll find the date of the hearing inside this envelope."

"Wha—what is this?"

"It's a PFA, sir."

"A what?"

"A restraining order. The details can be found inside. Sign this please."

I sign the form he hands me, take the envelope from him. I tear it open, let go of the hold I have on my door, letting it swing away from me.

Reading the thing brings back the sound of Kelly hitting the floor. I hear it over and over again, the blood beating in my ears as I run over the same printed lines for the second and third time. My forehead beads with sweat. My eyes water. I suck back something wet in my nose.

"Sir?" the cop says.

"I'm good. I'm shocked, but—"

"No, sir. What's that?"

He's staring over my shoulder. I turn, see my helmet sitting on the coffee table, a felt rag and spray oil next to it.

"Motorcycle helmet," I say.

"In an accident recently?"

"Yes, sir," I say holding a hand up, displaying the wrecked knuckles I got from punching through a car window.

"It's an interesting design."

"It's new."

"Yeah?"

"Yep."

"Mind if I come in, take a look at it? I ride too."

"I don't think that's the greatest idea, Officer..."

"Norton."

"Officer Norton. Sorry, but I think you should go now. Thank you for serving me."

Norton smiles, backs away from the door, says, "Have a nice night."

"You too."

He walks down the hall, and I keep an eye on him the entire way to the elevator. He turns, says, "Hey, make sure to lock your windows, okay?"

"Sure, thanks."

"There's a nut in a mask running around beating the hell out of people. Can't be too careful."

"Thanks for the tip."

The elevator dings, the doors roll open. He stands there staring, smiling for a moment, then waves.

Closing the door, I read the words on the PFA over and over again. The words telling me I am no longer allowed within one hundred yards of Kelly or her family outside of the hearing that will take place in a month.

I lift my helmet from the coffee table, look into the empty eye sockets.

Without buffing out the scrape on the forehead I buckle it onto my head and get dressed.

• • •

The house is dark. Too dark to see anything more than my reflection through the skylight, my own featureless face staring back through black eyes. My breath catches in my throat.

The glass cutter I keep in my belt is in my hand. I can't remember reaching for it. Or clicking it open. But I scratch the blade along the frame of the pane anyway. Making sure the glass doesn't fall inside, I wedge the blade into a cut corner to lift it from its mooring. I lift, set the pane aside, and drop myself inside after checking for anyone waiting in the dark.

The furniture hasn't been used for a day or two. The indents normally present have filled out.

I walk through the darkness listening as my breathing becomes stressed. My chest doesn't fully expand, my vision gets spotty from the lack of oxygen, and the helmet becomes more a prison than protection. So I pull it off, try to suck as much air down as I can.

I keep a small flashlight in my belt, but my fingers shake too much to undo the clasp to the compartment it's kept in. My knees are weak. My steps feeble and uncertain.

They're gone.

In the kitchen I walk over the spot where Kelly landed, force the sound away. There's nothing in the sink, or the dishwasher. Or the refrigerator. The flowers are gone.

I move from the kitchen to the dining room, to the library with its books all in their proper place. I walk up the stairs, careful to be silent for no reason, maneuver around the motorized chair on the track bolted into the wall.

The bathroom is clean, no tube of toothpaste lying rolled up on the sink, no hair products, no soap, no towels hanging on a hook or a door knob.

The floorboards under the carpet groan as I walk the hallway passing an office without a computer on the desk, a spare bedroom, the master with the bed made.

Kelly's door is closed, but opens with a push. It's perfect, sterile. Almost as if it's waiting for the dust to settle.

I sit on her bed trying to breathe. But I can't. Even after pulling my helmet off, the air I'm trying to suck back doesn't move much further than my throat. It gets caught there and coughed back up. Blood pulses in my temples as my heart ramps up its pace. I slip from the bed. On my hands and knees, drawing hiccupped breaths, my mouth hangs open, a wire of saliva runs from my lip to the floor.

• • •

Officer Norton, inside my apartment, stares at me through my window. I'm on my fire escape, but its dark enough that he can't see me. There's no lighting out here, and the street lights below don't help his vision. He doesn't know he's looking at anything but his own reflection in the window.

The cops are rooting through my closet. They're cataloging things that could possibly prove I am what Norton thinks I am. They'll find dark clothing, emergency medical supplies, receipts for bouquets I had sent to Kelly's, students' progress reports. And the carpet cleaner. Everything else I'm wearing. Anything incriminating I disposed of. Norton's hunch based on my carelessness will become nothing more than a wasted night for his precinct.

Norton presses the butts of his palms to the window, cups his hands and looks through. I hear him say what the fuck.

I don't move. I only realize that I'm hyperventilating again when he puts his ear to the window.

Then he opens it.

And I'm over the fire escape railing before Norton tosses off some compulsory cop word. My ankle pops, slick and wet, when I hit the sidewalk. My knee buckles. My spine sends a shockwave of pain shooting from my tailbone to the base of my skull. My stitches tear open.

But I get up, move a fast I as can, make my way to the alley where I dumped all the biohazardous waste from the other night.

I get tunnel vision from the pain. My eyes twist the street into a spiral of concrete and metal. I set a car alarm off, smashing through a side-view mirror.

Then there are cops yelling for me. Shouting commands at something they can't see.

I turn left, stumble down an alley. Hitting Van Pelt Street and turning back toward the direction of my building, I collapse at the side of a dumpster, crawl behind it.

I wait here for the cops' voices to fade.

• • •

The pain clouds my vision, but I can stand. I can hobble. The last of the flashing lights from a police cruiser came and went a while ago. The sirens have stopped. I shimmy my way from behind the dumpster and walk. Never stepping into a streetlamp's light, I work my way behind parked cars, sticking as close to walls as possible. The blocks blur into neighborhoods as I move, hiding from everything, making sure I'm unseen.

I walk until I can't anymore. Until my legs, weak and broken, collapse under my weight.

I reach for something to pull myself from the ground. But my hands find nothing. My lungs tighten, my breaths shorten. My heartbeat pulses in my ears, pumping louder with each beat.

Until I hear a different sound.

A whimpering from down the street.

I crawl toward it.

Around the corner, a man presses a woman up against a wall, holds his hand over her mouth. He tells her this will only take a minute.

She begs him to let her go. I hear her begin to cry.

I stand, move toward them.

He sees me before I reach them. He pulls a gun, points it at me, tells me to walk away.

"I can't," I say.

"The fuck you can't. Get out of here."

So I run.

Directly at him.

He pulls the trigger. I hear the shots, but don't feel anything. I'm used to the pain.

On the ground, with the guy under me, fighting me, I wait. I wait until I see her running away. Until I hear the sound of her shoes hitting the pavement, getting as far away from me as she can.

Muncy

Claire never wished Franklin dead. But she often imagined what life would be like were he to not return home from a shift. What she would do. Where she would go. If she would find out if the issue was her or Franklin.

Sometimes Franklin would be late, forget to call and tell her so. She'd sit, watch the television, read a book, bore herself staring at the computer screen in the spare room. Then panic until he'd come home.

Lately, Claire had figured that every call that came through was someone from the station to tell her Franklin had gone and gotten himself killed. Clipped off the side of the road writing a ticket. Stabbed underneath his vest with a buck knife clearing out a fight at the Muncy Pub. Shot through the eye during a standoff down the center of town.

But Muncy was mostly drunk drivers running down mailboxes or driving into the front of Metz' tool shed round the blind spot on 83. Breaking and entering. Domestic disputes. Everything else was in bigger towns in bigger counties surrounding bigger cities, places Claire wished she lived. Franklin would tell her so over a beer on good nights—over two, three, four on bad ones.

Regardless, the shift from panic and paranoia to violent fantasy had become permanent. Took root as Claire would tell herself to stop it, just stop it.

With the news talking about more rain, Claire, foggy from her head pills, heard Franklin creak through the screen door on the porch, scrape his boots on the nailed down mud chucker. She stubbed out her cigarette, sat up on the couch, brushed away the ashes that drifted down the front of her robe.

Franklin stepped in, said hello, then sorry, then he went to the fridge for his beer.

Claire said, "Long night?"

With his head behind the refrigerator door, Franklin said, "Dispute down south end of Cranston's property. Some idiot shot the dog and said he thought it was a bear."

Claire imagined Franklin's obit were he shot by accident down Cranston's. The wording. The photograph. The term she'd give herself. Widow or wife.

Franklin stood up straight, closed the fridge door. Hanging off one side his face, torn, bloody, showing the white nub of bone, his jaw swung back and forth while he spoke about the type of stupidity it takes to mistake Mr. Cranston's old black lab for a bear. Then he asked, "What's the matter?" his face mended and whole.

Hand on her chest, mouth open, Claire said, "What?"

"You're looking at me like I grew me a second head."

Claire, stuck in her permanent couch indent, said, "I suppose my mind played a trick on me."

On the television was a report about a homicide far enough away not to matter.

"Well, shit," Franklin said, "Let's watch something other than the damn news then, huh?"

Franklin kissed Claire's cheek, sat beside her in his own ass imprint, turned on something else.

• • •

Franklin encouraged Claire every so often to go on out and find something to fill her time with. Told her it's not good having nothing to do but wait home. But most of Claire's friends had children or had more on the way. They'd looked at her sideways when she'd said she didn't care much for babies. Or the thought of having one. Or the thought of pushing one out of herself. She couldn't very well call them up for a chat. Her single friends had gone and left Muncy all together once it started falling apart.

Her teaching certificate had expired a few years after the high school closed down. The only other jobs in town—waiting tables at the Soanes' Inn, tending bar at the Muncy Pub—she'd gotten fired from on account of her being damn awful at them and not caring enough to get better.

Franklin's not wanting to leave his hometown, Claire's want to get out and go anywhere else had led to daytime television, cigarettes, the shit computer with the lousy DSL, and paperback novels bought from the collapsing supermarket just past the grassed-over railroad tracks.

Claire took the last of her pills, spent the morning writing letters to Franklin. Letters about how unhappy she was living in a ghost town. Letters about her love for him not being enough to continue living the way she was. Letters about the things she'd been keeping from him.

She balled them all up, took them out back and burned them. Figured it'd be better not to destroy Franklin with just her chicken scratch.

She drove miles out of town, down the highway, past the rusted empty factories, through a tunnel until a city rose up from the horizon.

Driving, she practiced what she was going to say over the phone whenever she stopped wherever she was headed. "Frank, I want a divorce—no—Franky, I need a divorce—no—You're a wonderful man, Frank, but I'm...goddammit."

She thought of his face, red and melting in grief.

She thought of the sounds he would make, wet sobbing and whimpers.

She thought of him killing himself, putting his gun in his mouth.

The car drifted over a rumble strip, but Claire jerked the wheel left just before she got the chance to slam into a bridge abutment.

Further down the highway she drafted a big rig, could read the registration sticker on the license plate, waited for brake lights, waited for her car to cram itself underneath the tires.

She imagined plowing through the cement wall on the bridge past Stanton, the car nose-diving into the valley, exploding when it hit bottom.

Instead she eased the car off the highway at the next exit, made her way back to the onramp and headed on back toward Muncy. The only one who would care if she'd gone and died would be that poor dumb boy, Franklin. And he didn't deserve that.

She regretted thinking him dumb. Simple and happy, he deserved the kindnesses he'd given.

She decided to run the errands she'd planned on never running again.

At her last stop, a pharmacy just outside Dunlop, the pharmacist smiled at her, said hello.

Claire did the same, said, "How you been?"

"Same ol' same ol', you know? No one ever told me life would be so boring."

"Could be worse, I suppose."

"Could be, sure. Boring job, you know how it goes."

Claire said nothing.

"But sometimes I think quitting would be nice."

Claire asked for her prescriptions.

The pharmacist went to the back, pulled two noisy white paper bags from the shelf, handed them over to her.

Claire gave a shot at a smile but turned, said thanks and left. She drove home and waited for Franklin's shift to end.

• • •

Franklin came home early, asked Claire if she wanted to try again.

Afterward, Claire showered, took her pills—one for her brain, one for her lady parts—and hid them deep down in her otherwise useless travel kit. Then she went back to the bedroom to find Franklin still nude, sleeping on top of the covers.

She watched him a bit. His chest rising, falling, his breaths turning into snotty snoring.

He'd left his work clothes on the floor next to the bed. His duty rig and gun at the top of the heap instead of hanging from the doorknob where he usually left them.

He was a sweet man. Dopey. A little chubby. But kind, funny. He liked how much Claire read, told her so back when they first were married. He'd said marrying a smart woman made him feel smarter. He was never smart. He only knew things he knew and everything else was Claire's territory.

But Claire couldn't call herself smart. Not anymore.

She imagined coming home from a job she liked, from a job that don't exist, finding Franklin on the bed, riddled with bullet holes. Someone he had once put away had been released from prison, went to find him, murdered him in his sleep. Unloaded Franklin's own service weapon into his chest, gut, and balls.

Franklin farted, woke himself up. He scratched his belly, blinked sleep away, said, "Honey?"

"Just getting up to shower."

Franklin said okay, turned over, fell back to sleep quick.

Claire smoked cigarettes and drank Franklin's beer until she fell asleep on the couch.

Varied and increasingly grisly fantasies of Franklin's end drove Claire to flush her Effexor down the shitter. Then she stopped going to her therapist after she couldn't bring herself to tell him that Franklin's death was occupying most of her waking thoughts. And her dreams. And when she wasn't thinking of Franklin dying she was thinking of drowning herself. Shooting herself. Setting herself on fire.

During her last session, Claire had said she felt the medication was doing something funny to her. That it was making her feel awful things about Franklin who had never done nothing to her but let her settle into boredom and depression—not that it was ever his responsibility.

She'd said, "I don't exist."

Said, "I'm nothing."

Said, "Nobody would notice if I just up and left."

Her therapist asked, "Why not just leave then, Claire? Start over if you're so unhappy?"

"I can't. Franklin's a good man. Doesn't deserve that kind of pain."

"Then you need to let the medicine do its job—which takes time—or you need to get up the courage to change."

Claire hadn't been back since.

She took long drives most days after that. One day she went so far she got home later than Franklin.

He'd asked where she'd gone when she got home, the back of his skull gone, chunks of brain slopping down onto the couch as he spoke.

Her eyes stung. She blinked away tears, said, "I'm trying to get myself something to do."

"Well then I think that's great. But leave a note for me next time, okay? Damn scared me half to death."

Claire sat next to Franklin, lit a cigarette. She started to cry. Nearly lit her hair on fire, cigarette still pinched between her fingers.

Franklin wrapped his arm around her shoulders, asked what was wrong. Said he can't do anything to help if she won't tell him what's got her all spun about. Said she needs to calm down so they can talk.

Claire wept longer than she thought she needed to. Wondered if it was genuine, or some deep down intention to lie.

Franklin asked, "What is it, Claire? What's going on?"

Claire sucked back on her runny nose, couldn't think of anything to say, but said, "I want a baby, Frank. I want a baby so bad."

"Maybe we should try and talk to one of them baby doctors?"

"Maybe." Claire took Franklin's hand, stood, led him into the bedroom.

• • •

Their appointment with the specialist was set for a week from Wednesday.

During the week leading up to it, Claire kept taking her pill. Kept venturing further away from Muncy every day. Kept bedding Franklin to make up for almost not coming home most days.

But she started drinking up most of the beer in the house.

Sick and guilty by day, drunk and horny by night, Claire got careless. Left lit cigarettes in the ashtray until they were nothing but a butt and a straw of gray dust. Misplaced things. Neglected things. Microwaved old frozen dinners. Used tissues in place of the toilet paper she neglected to buy when she was out every day.

The Monday before the appointment she walked down to the Muncy Pub, sat, drank, and waited for someone to say hello. She drank until she stood, said, "None of you motherfuckers would miss me if I left, huh?"

They asked her real nice to leave.

Tuesday she drove straight through two counties, planned not to go back, for sure this time.

She did ninety most the way down the highway hoping for a tire to blow and flip the car. Or a deer to jump out onto the road and send her flying through the windshield. Or a piece of rebar to break loose from a truck hauling bundles of the stuff and impale her through the mouth, out the back of her head.

She pulled over hyperventilating, crying, thinking of Franklin getting home to an empty house, waiting for her to come home, sitting there until he died, rotted, turned to dust.

If she was going to leave him she'd at least tell him to his face. Kind, but honest. Maybe give him the option to come with her. But she was leaving with or without him. She practiced her speech all the way home to keep from turning to chickenshit.

She got home after dark. After Franklin.

He'd left all the lights on. Left the television on. Left a trail of beer cans from the coffee table to the armchair to the bedroom.

The bedroom door was open a crack from the weight of Franklin's rig hanging from the doorknob on the other side.

Lit by the lights from the living room, lying on the bed, Franklin laid on his back in spilt beer, the overturned empty can next to his hand.

Claire said, "Frank."

He didn't move.

Claire wondered if he'd drunk himself to death.

He scratched his belly.

Claire almost reached to shake him awake, almost said she had something she needed to talk with him about.

Then she saw the blister pack of her pills on the end table.

She imagined him finding them. Using the computer in the spare room to look up the brand name. Crying. Drinking. Passing out drunk as piss, wrecked, betrayed.

Claire backed into the door, heard Franklin's gun clunk against the wood.

Crying she reached for the pistol, pulled it from the holster.

She cocked the gun, put the barrel in her mouth, tasted the metal and oil.

He'd find her, blame himself. He'd resent her, hate himself for it. He'd live alone, die alone, get found because of the smell.

Claire pulled the gun barrel from between her teeth.

She walked toward Franklin.

His mouth open, snoring, Claire cried for him. Regretted lying to the dimwit. Regretted marrying the fool.

She aimed the gun at his face.

Then she pulled the trigger.

She watched Franklin's brains spray down her pillow, a clump of hair, blood and bone flop onto the headboard.

Claire took Franklin's rig with her. She loaded her car with things she thought she'd need. Ignored the neighbor across the creek asking what had happened. She cried again pulling away from the house, but knew Franklin was better now not having to know everything she'd felt. She drove past the Soane's Inn, the Muncy Pub, the police station, and clear out of Muncy. She left the county, crossed into another, drove through a tunnel. There was red and blue in her rearview, but a city was on the horizon, lit up and blocking out the stars.

Stars & Star Maps

She says they're too many. She can't count them. Can't feel them either.

But, possibility. The rocks spinning around them, the things clinging to the stone without doing anything but living there—if they're there.

She says it's too big. Everything. This, here, now, she believes in all of it. Out there makes down here nothing.

But, out there is down here. It's all part of the same something. Something, maybe not important, but heavy.

She says, "Hear that?"

Wind rushing through the grass.

She says, "Feel that?"

Fingerprints over goose pimples.

She says, "I'd rather they watch this."

Love & Marriage & Love & Marriage

The room's well lit, colorful. There's wainscoting and crown moulding and polished brass doorknobs. The hardwoods glisten from the light coming through the windows.

Working on set every day, though, you notice the gaudiness. The colors that only look good on film. The fireplace bricks, oily-looking up close because they're plastic. The too-bright stage lights that are just bright enough to prove they're fake.

Not fake-fake.

Just not all the way real.

You feel not fake-fake too as you burst through the door to a cheering live studio audience because your face is flush and your belly's too big. To cameras all aimed at you, sitting on electrical tape X's just beyond where the room's been cut in half. To the director with his script rolled up like a giant cigarette. And you're like, Goddamn you wish you had a cigarette.

That's your line. Without the goddamn.

"I wish I had a cigarette," you say.

And the crowd laughs and cheers at your catchphrase.

It's edgy humor. Cigarettes are edgy now and a pregnant lady being that sort of edgy is funny.

In real life, people would be appalled. Maybe.

But there's nothing real about any of this.

Your husband Brian, whose arc this season has turned him into a real dumbass, kicks his way into the living room from across the set. He stands up straight, puts his fists to his hips, gives you a look, and says, "Cigarettes make your hair smell like my Gamgam."

Cue laughter.

Cue long pause before next line to let laughter linger.

Then Brian says, "And I'd rather not think of Gam-Gam while we're doing it. Even though you're totally as big as she is now."

You're staring, thinking, Jesus how can these writers sleep at night after writing this stuff. Thinking, Oh shit I have something I'm supposed to say. Thinking, you'll ask to be written off. You'll die in childbirth. They'll make it funny.

You exaggerate an eye roll, use your head, play up the body language. Then you say, "Gam-Gam's dead."

"What?" Brian says.

"Remember? We told her we were pregnant at her ninetieth birthday party? An embolism burst in her brain? She went face-first into ninety lit birthday candles and set her blue wig on fire?"

Brian waits for the crowd to settle.

Then he laughs, says, "Oh yeah. Well you're certainly hotter than a fat old corpse."

Cue laughter.

Cue contraption strapped to your crotch being remotely set off to soak your elastic waist-banded sweatpants-jeans.

Cue Brian telling you, you peed yourself, his face all wrinkled-sick.

Then you cringe because you know you have the worst line that's ever been written for you. Edgy humor your ass. Whatever happened to subtlety? To privacy. To modesty. To your body being a vessel for your particular brand of comedy instead of a thing that went from size zero to preggers over the break in the shooting schedule to get people watching again.

Your face goes red before you say it, and when you say it you can almost taste it. "Just wait until I start pushing. I've been constipated for three days."

Brian sells it. Looks confused. As if he hadn't read the script at all. As if he doesn't know that all the jokes in the delivery room scene are about nipples, and vaginas, and buttholes. Because really, everything'll be hanging out and up for grabs. And everybody'll be poking and prodding. And Brian'll pass out on a big foam mat and get a big laugh while you have to scream and curse and make jokes about shitting yourself in front of an audience.

But that's the job, isn't it?

That's what you're supposed to do.

Be a good sport. Don't be difficult. You don't want to be one of those actresses.

Brian'll never have the pleasure of having a room full of people pretend to stare up into him. He'll never know what it's like to be made into a waddling, gassy, nine-episode joke to make the studio execs all happy during Sweeps Week.

You know what it's taken to get here. You followed everybody's advice. Did everything right. Eked out your own corner of network television.

Then the ratings drop, the writers quit, the critics get flat-out mean, and you have to compromise to keep this thing going. Whatever this thing is anymore.

Brain's not Brian.

They barely use the bedroom set anymore.

You always feel like shit and look like shit and feel like shit.

Then the laughter ends.

Brian says his line about poo-poo and hoo-hahs and gags a little, puts his hands on his knees saying oh god, oh god, he's not ready for this. And that's when you have to make your way across the set in wet-crotched pants to rub his back.

"It's okay," you say. "After all of it we'll come home with our little baby. That's like a dream come true, right?"

Brian stands, wraps his arms around your enormous body, and kisses you right on the lips.

The audience belts out a big, genuine aw-sound.

This Distance

When Brian pulls away from you he smiles, says, "We're having a baby."

You smile, nod yes, force your eyes glassy.

"We're having a baby," he says again, yanking the end of the sentence up into a question.

You say, "Brian?"

Then he collapses.

It'll make for a great promo shot.

On the next *Love & Marriage & Love & Marriage*...

Cut to your close-up after Brain's collapse.

"Does this mean I'm driving?"

Everybody knows what adding a baby to a show about a fun couple having sex and getting caught and failing to be adults means.

Rent the shark. Get the crew to build a ramp. Buy a boat, hire a stunt skier.

But it's a way to get people paying attention again after you run out of things for two people to do all cute and funny.

You'll get another season.

Two.

Maybe three if Brian's drunken, deadbeat sister is upgraded from recurring to regular.

But after that it'll be over.

The set that looks like a really nice place to live from the audience seats will be dismantled. The crew will be assigned to other shows almost identical to this one. Brian will probably never work again because he won't want to play stupid anymore. And once you pull this Velcro baby suit off you can do shampoo commercials and prepare for cancellation.

You'll move on. Maybe to a soap for a while.

Then more than likely you'll age out of all the good roles.

And, if you're lucky, you'll get a spot on a daytime talk show that gets ignored most days and mocked on late night TV every now and then.

But for now, before the director yells cut and you have to hump it over to the hospital set to be sprayed down and draped in a paper gown, there's a smiling, cheering audience who thinks you're great.

They're so happy for your character.

Everyone loves a baby.

For a little while you'll be fine with Brian and everything'll be new and funny again.

And really, in this business there's not much else you could ask for.

The Beyond

Jordan has two hours before she has to step into the Beyond. She says she wants to go for a walk to pass the time. We haven't been on a walk together since she applied for her portal date just after her status changed to terminal. I've been more worried than she's been through this entire process. And now I'm more worried about how she'll feel bouncing about the still, white dust outside.

We both put on weight after the wedding. You say you won't, but you do.

She's since lost all of hers. More.

If I didn't know any better I could swear that I see her pale bony hips and shoulders through her pressure suit. It hangs baggy around her breasts, her butt, her belly. But she's not that thin, can't be that thin. I'm certainly not. My suit pinches me in all the places hers leaves to the imagination. In the cold black I'm afraid all the weight I've put on will split my suit open, send me spinning through space like a balloon through the air back home. But I know that couldn't really happen just as I know I can't see Jordan's bones through her suit, just as I know the Beyond will be good for her.

She said Heaven used to work for some people, but the Beyond is indisputable fact.

Told me that it'll be good for her.

She struggles with the zippers, magnetic clasps, and straps on the back of her suit.

I don't help her, keep checking that the maglocks on my boots are glowing green for connected. But when she asks for a little help please, her voice a bit curved toward snappy, I can't help but breathe out some relief. I buckle, snap, zip, and secure with my lips pursed into a tiny smile that I know she knows is there, but says nothing about.

After Jordan got her Beyond date I'd waited for her to ask me for something, anything. Helping only when she needed me. All proud of myself for not forcing my way into things she felt she could still do herself. So we've kept conversations mostly pleasant since. But there were plenty of nights I holed myself up in the bathroom and turned into a sniveling wreck until she knocked on the door and asked me to watch all the promotional materials with her again, to help her please.

The way the science works is definitive, accurate.

Cold.

But the short film was mesmerizing. Everything was shiny. Everyone was sick but smiling. And we were told everything would be just fine. Jordan would step through a portal into a collective soul of humanity in a pocket dimension that exists outside time and space and houses all human energy that was ever created ever. She'd be her and she'd be everyone and everyone would be her and so on and so forth, like a quantum physics funhouse. She'd be more at home than she'd ever been.

After the video, Jordan asked me what I was thinking. All I could do was nod, tell her how lovely everything seemed. I did my best, kept the tears in, my bottom lip from shaking, my stomach from turning itself inside out. She was going and I had to be brave and make her feel like everything was going to be okay and show her that I would be fine one day and that I was looking forward to following her through the portal when it was my time. Sick or old, whichever came first.

Now, buckling her helmet, under two hours left, the lines on her face are deep, the bags under her eyes are dark, her lips look like they'd never been pink a day in her life, and I'm asking her where we should go on our walk with a smile. I say Tycho, or

Wargentin, or Stöfler. When Jordan tells me to pick I say Tycho because that's the first place we visited after we moved up here. It's a tiny little town at the bottom of the crater. Shops lining the walking paths with signs inviting us to come on in through the airlocks and try the solar system's famous Martian chai tea, or zero G-raised cattle steaks, or fresh moon-soil potatoes.

Jordan smiles, nods in her fishbowl helmet, says, "Your favorite."

I cock an eyebrow, laugh a little. "Our favorite, remember?"

"I remember."

We leave our apartment pod through the back airlock so we won't have to waddle our way down the road, around the corner through the no leaping zone.

Outside is stars over our heads, billions of billions of them, and soft white under our feet stretching from our colony to the next in long fields of foot-printed perfect, clean dirt. Jordan, through my earpiece, breathes deep, lets it go. Then she looks to Earth. That big blue, white orb that our kids, if we'd had enough time to have them, would've figured is the Moon's moon. And before I can ask if she's ready for this, Jordan bends her knees and flings herself into open space, the retrorockets on her boots firing a bolt of light. She floats up, up, up, slowing as gravity regains its light grip on her. For a moment, a second, she hangs up there, the sun catching the glass on her helmet, and I'm breathing heavy and deep with my heart beating in my temples.

When Jordan lands she asks me if I'm okay, if I'm having an attack.

I don't answer. I jump into space.

The stars are bright and white and glittering, but I can't look at them. Can't be bothered with them. Jordan shrinking away below me and I'm supposed to admire things that have been around for a billion years. Doesn't make a whole lot of sense. Not really. Because if science has told us anything about them it's confirmed that most of the stars we spend so much time gazing at are already dead and gone. So I keep my eyes on Jordan through my puffy, red-faced reflection in my fishbowl as I reach the top of my arc, stall, and fall

Jordan's always been more graceful than me. She always lands on the surface, bends her knees, takes, one, two, three steps and comes to a stop. I collapse into the white, flip, bounce off my back, my front, and come to a sliding stop on my butt. Over the radio Jordan asks am I okay, am I okay. I turn, smile, give a thumbs-up, and almost laugh at the trail of dust clouds hanging feet off the ground that leads to Jordan as she heads my way.

Jordan has tried so hard to make me believe she's doing fine. She never slowed down. Kept going to work. Kept helping around the house. She even took care of my laundry after I'd forgotten for two weeks and wore the same underwear and socks to work three days in a row. She even made me dinner on days when work was awful enough that I wouldn't say anything when I got home besides hello, besides how are you, besides good, great to hear. She even started going with me to my own doctor's appointments just to listen to me talk about how I'm feeling so she could better understand.

Now I tell her I'm okay, I'm okay as I dust moon gravel off my suit. One hand on my bicep the other on my air pack on my back, she asks me if I'm sure. Sure-sure. Really sure.

"I'm sure," I say.

"I don't know if you are," Jordan says, her breath fogging up the glass in front of her mouth.

"Why do you say that?" I say.

"You worry me sometimes."

I take Jordan's fishbowl between my gloved, pressurized hands, say, "You don't have to worry about me."

We say nothing for a while, then continue our bouncing walk toward Tycho.

Our first night out after we settled in up here was at a little Tycho pub named for what it was. I'd heard it had good soup, the best burgers. We'd decided to meet there after work. I was late like always. I kissed her when I showed up, then blamed everything else for why I wasn't on time. Goddamn airlock at work. The shit rover I'd gotten on the cheap—should've just walked. The parking lot attendant wouldn't take credits—no one carries chips anymore.

She smiled, ordered me a drink, stared at me while I spoke long enough that I started feeling self-conscious. Like there was gunk in the corner of my eye, or something hanging from my nose.

Then she laughed a little. Drank from her bottle. Shushed me.

When my beer came I asked her who did she think she was shushing.

She did it again. And we laughed.

We forgot about the soup, the burgers, just kept drinking, laughing, drinking after that. Enough drinking that Jordan took the keys to the rover from me outside, stuffed them into her pressure suit pocket.

"I'll have to pay for the night," I said.

She rolled her eyes, said, "I feel like if I weren't here you'd drive home, take a hill too fast and fling yourself and the rover off into space."

"Piece of shit deserves it."

"Yeah, but you don't."

"Don't you talk about my rover like that."

We waddled home talking, laughing, talking.

Now, the pub's closed.

We stand out front. I'm knocking on the airlock widow, staring through it. All the chairs upside down on the tables. The lights dimmed. The televisions off. The taps covered.

Through my earpiece Jordan tells me they're not opening for another hour. I'm pounding on the window saying if they knew the circumstances they'd open for us, I just need to get someone's attention. I punch the window again and again until Jordan takes my other hand, says, it's okay, it's okay all tinny and distant.

Through her helmet her forehead's wrinkled, her eyes are wide and glassy, she's saying something but my coms go in and out. All I hear is, "You're...out...time..."

I say, "Say again? What?"

"It's...over...go."

"What? What's that?"

"...still got time."

Before I can ask her what again my ass is in the dirt and I'm breathing but not really. I check my O2 levels, all the hoses running from my tank to my filters to my helmet. They're all fine, but I'm sucking down nothing, feeling my eyeballs bulge out of their sockets.

Jordan, she tells me to relax, her voice coming in loud and clear now. Following me up the road, she says it's not my suit, it's me, and I need to concentrate on her voice.

Her voice saying, "Shh."

Saying, "You're okay, you'll be okay."

Saying, "Look where you are. It'll be some life."

Between the moon's dusty surface, Earth hanging over us, spinning, spinning, and a sky-full of stars all reflected on and around Jordan's face in the glass, more air makes its way into my lungs breath after breath. The first one of these I'd had I was able to get over myself. Each one after that turned from panic to complete lunacy to wall-punching violence. Until Jordan worked out the techniques that could bring me back.

Focus on something else.

A voice.

An image.

Something that'll pull me out.

I tell her I'm good. Please not to look at me that way, I swear I'm fine.

But all I can think of is the Beyond when she walks up the slight crater slope, drops to the ground, sits in a cloud of moon dust clunking a gloved hand on her helmet like she was hoping she could use it to clear her eyes. The Beyond. The place I can't go yet. The place I'll watch her dissolve into her most basic parts soon. Atoms, protons, neutrons, electrons, all the bits I can't see that made the soul I've followed around for the better part of a decade.

If I push past the scientists in their lab coats and black goggles, manage to widen the portal to fit two, or even ask why the fuck can't I fucking go with her, maybe I could go too. But even as a multidimensional wavelength of celestial intent, Jordan would never let me live that one down. It's not for healthy people, she'd say. Somebody else needed it, not you, she'd say. For infinity.

Sitting next to Jordan, our helmets keep our heads from each other's shoulders. But it's the thought. And it works.

We sit a while, watch people make their way through the Tycho streets. Maybe on their way home from work. Maybe heading out for the night somewhere fancy for dinner, somewhere dingy for booze and cigarettes. And Jordan's sniffling becomes more and more infrequent until she pushes away from me, struggles to her feet.

I look away, try to not react to the small sounds she makes in her throat with the pain shooting through her as she moves.

She says hey, breathing heavy. "Look at me."

Her hand reaches down for me to take. "Come on."

I get up slow, hope that it makes Jordan feel that she's helping me even though she and I both know she barely has strength enough to pull the refrigerator door open anymore.

Standing, facing her, through my earpiece she says, "Hold on."

I reach around her helmet, rest my arms on her pack.

She wraps her arms around my ribs, my belly smiles, eyes all shiny and wet.

And then we're five feet off the ground, ten feet, twenty.

Below, when the light from Jordan's retrorockets blinks out, a cloud of dust, all of Tycho. And we're still floating up, up, up with the momentum. All around, there's nothing but me, Jordan, and a black, sparkling curtain of space.

When we reach the top of our arc, there's that pause. That moment between gravities. Suspension. No push or pull from anything. Just Jordan and me and black. Just before the Moon tells us enough's enough.

We use the retrorockets to slow us down, land on the dusty surface without a sound.

Jordan doesn't look me in the eyes, hides hers, looks past me. "The bar's open," she says.

I grab her arm before she can walk away. Tell her to wait. Say we should go again.

And then we're blasting off into space. Stuck in the in-between for one minute, two, three. And when we're up there, star maps on our faces, I'm breathing fine. Jordan's face isn't angled and creased, her eyebrows aren't cocked, her forehead's not wrinkled. Her tired, bloodshot eyes are wide open. Like they used to be.

Just before we go back up a third time, an alarm goes off in our earpieces.

Jordan says, "I have to go."

She lets go of me, waddle-walks away back toward Tycho's town center.

"Just wait," I say.

I wrap her up, tell her to hold on, and we're up in the black again.

Tycho spins away beneath us. Earth gets larger above us even though I know it doesn't, not really. I hear her through my earpiece. I see her through two layers of starry glass. And I'm the one saying things that Jordan would say to me.

I'm carrying her for once.

We're going up, up, up.

And when we're in that nothing space I keep us pushing through it.

We don't have enough momentum to go anywhere. Not really. This—wherever this is—it'll lose its hold on us. Soon enough. But with bolts of light under my feet, with Jordan still here, and with enough fuel to stay suspended for however long, we're not going anywhere.

Not for a while.

The Beyond can wait.

Me and You on Regis-132

There's a planet just like ours. But nothing like ours.

Regis-132 is fourteen hundred light years away. Or so.

And right now, through our telescopes, we're staring at its past. Whatever, whoever was there will have lived, died, and been absorbed into planet's atoms to make something new. Something spectacular.

Of course, from here it just looks like another space rock. Like here does from there.

But it's different.

Much.

And we, me and you, we can go there. We can go there for good. For an ending.

We'll rip a hole in spacetime, step through the tear, and come out on the other side with nothing but you, me, and a planet named after Regis Philbin, but not really named after Regis Philbin—you know my sense of humor. Or lack thereof as you say with a smile and a finger to my love-handles.

Think about it.

It's like this.

We're old. Earth's gravity's hard on our bones.

Over there we'll weigh a quarter less than we do right now. We'll be able to jump and float and land nice and soft in the purple, downy grass. More dandelion seeds than grass. Less allergies than dandelion seeds.

Think about it.

It's like this.

We're finished. No jobs. No debt. No kids. We're not beholden to anyone or anything on this planet anymore. And even when we were, did any of it really matter? Really. The short answer would probably be more of a combination of Yes and No, the longer answer would make things all shimmery with nostalgia, bitter with regret.

Over there. there's no history. No human history anyway. Not a single blue, green, red, or purple-glowing native will have anything to hold against us. They won't come around asking us why we haven't come back to the newly-rebuilt church even though you can still smell the ash in the air around it. They won't stare at us gliding down the anti-gravity streets like we're planning to do something to them despite our canes, our grays, our plastic shoes. They won't ever tell us how well-spoken we are, won't wonder about whether or not our degrees are legitimate, won't dare say they're the ones who are underrepresented.

They're super-advanced lifeforms who travel the starways in fantastic, faster-than-light ships. No way else to do that than having their heads on right. Or wherever-they-keep-their-brains on right. Makes sense their society works just as well as a Twin Miniature-Blackhole-Powered Spectrum Engine.

Think about it.

It's like this.

It's more likely we'll be gunned down than die of your smoker's cough or my early-stage Dementia. On the street. Or at a restaurant. Or on a bus. Or on a traffic stop. Or in our own damn house. Because if nothing else things have gotten worse and life for you and me has gotten more tenuous. And it's not about a fear of dying at this age. It's more a fear of how I'm going to die and how my death will be misinterpreted.

Over there, because of the technologies that allow buildings to stand so high, you can see them from orbit—the pinnacles poking out into the black of space—wonderment is more important than anything else. Than property. Than money. Than some ridiculous sense of self-defense.

Wouldn't that be something?

To go outside every day and just marvel.

At the trees that are more or less giant mushrooms that perfume the sky with pink mist every hour pollinating animal-flowers and making everyone smell like cotton candy.

At the skyways that weave through the cities, over the red forests, and bring everyone to their front doors in seconds through the Spectrum Tubing.

At the soft rainbow glow of a population unafraid to be outside at whatever time.

The view of Regis-132 from space is more a pulsating infinite-colored atom, the buildings and tubing and people making the view something everyone could only hope to ever see before they die.

Think about it.

It's like this.

You'll go outside and be astounded.

You'll go outside and cry over beautiful things.

You'll go outside.

You'll walk through that hole in spacetime we've ripped open with exploding hadrons. You'll feel that nervous flutter in your belly you get during the exciting parts of fantasy movies. You'll be bathed in the orange light of that Spectral Class K sun that'll be warm but not too warm all the time. And then I'll come through and together we'll shake hands with all sorts of people who won't be put off by us because differences are treasured there.

Think about it.

It's like this.

We'll walk through that portal, me and you, together.

We'll live with dignity, me and you, together.

And we'll end, me and you, together, as foreigners from a land that is eating itself, in a home our neighbors will have helped us build, smiling at all of the colors shimmering through the windows as we pass.

Lost in Space

I tell Dad I haven't gotten a response back yet.

He says to what.

"My script," I say.

"Oh. Right. How's school?"

Mom says my Dad's name, tells him to stop.

"Stop what?"

"Doing that to him."

They stare at each other across the table. Dad chews his food. Mom takes a sip of wine.

I sit there, knife and fork at the ready, waiting for something to happen. Someone to say something. I cut into my food instead. I cut the fat off the gray steak, pile it up at the edge of my plate. I mush mashed potatoes through the tines of my fork once, twice, but I recover in enough time to get Dad to stop watching me.

I tell Mom the food looks good.

She says thank you.

Dad says, "Stop playing with your food. It's weird."

Mom makes a hissing noise, cocks her eyebrow. She flicks her head toward me, keeping her eyes on Dad.

Dad raises his eyebrows, shrugs his shoulders.

Mom nods at me again, her eyes never separating from Dad's.

Dad says, "Which script is that?"

I skewer the fourth string bean onto my fork, hold it up, say, "Hmm?"

"The script you didn't hear back about."

I put the fork in my mouth, slide the string beans off on top of a mound of potatoes I smooshed between the underside of my tongue and bottom teeth. I'm careful to keep the greens in the same formation they entered before removing the fork.

I say, "It's a pilot for a new *Lost in Space* TV series."

Dad leans forward, says, "What?"

Mom says, "Finish that bite and say it again."

I swallow my food, tell Dad again about the script. About how I sent it to a whole slew of agents, producers, production companies. I tell him it's awesome.

"'Danger, danger, Will Robinson' *Lost in Space*?" he says.

I tell him there's only one. "You know that," I say.

He says he remembers it. Says, "Reruns on Sci-Fi Channel."

Mom says, "I loved that show."

I nod my head, spearing more string beans onto my fork.

"You're not going to eat your fat?" Dad says.

"Nope."

Dad reaches across the table and stabs each hunk of fat onto his fork, the metal clinking against the ceramic plate. It makes me flinch every time.

Mom says, "Careful."

"We don't waste food. Been telling him since he was a kid."

Once his fork is loaded with fat, Dad crams it all into his mouth. I can hear the gristle bursting, crunching between his teeth. He says, "How's school?"

I say, "I'm approaching it more as an exploratory series, more than the shoot-em-up style the movie went for back in '98."

Dad says my name.

"I like that movie, still," I say. "It doesn't hold up all that well, though. Which is a shame. I think it had real potential. I think it maybe just got stuck with a lousy director. Which hopefully won't happen with my series. Bad showrunner means bad show."

Dad says, "Milo." Louder this time.

I say, "I want to give it a tougher edge too. Give it a *Battlestar Galactica* treatment. Ramp up the drama, the interpersonal politics. Make it a little sexier. Maybe feature a love triangle between Major West, Dr. Robinson and Mrs. Doctor Robinson. I've also given them a skeleton crew to help with the—"

Dad slams his fist down on the table, silverware clatters, drinks spill. This time he yells my name.

Mom yells Dad's name.

Dad says, "Grace."

"Don't 'Grace' me," Mom says.

We sit there. Silent. Mom and Dad talk with their faces. I look back and forth, back and forth at them.

Without looking at me Dad says, "How. Is. School?"

I tell him it's great, that I get a lot of writing done. That a few of my professors think I'm a good storyteller.

Dad pushes his chair away from the table, says, "I'm full."

Mom stands up, says, "Sit down."

"No," Dad says. He says something about how this isn't normal. Says something about how I'm getting worse.

"He's our son," Mom says.

He says, "Yeah," walks past me through the living room. the television he shuts off a *Supernatural* rerun.

I'm threading the longer string beans into a weave pattern, scooping a dollop of potatoes on them and seeing if I can fit it into my mouth.

I hear the floorboards upstairs creek.

Mom refills her wine glass.

After a while I notice her staring at me. I say, "Sorry."

"It's fine. He'll be fine," she says. "Do you want to watch some *Firefly* before I drive you back?"

I tell her I do. But I don't think I'll enjoy it as much as I used to. Those guys are the reason I can't go to the New York Comic Con anymore. And I'm still a little sore about it.

• • •

When I was a kid I asked my dad if I could join Starfleet.

He told me I most definitely could. "But you have to be a grown up first," he said.

I asked him when that would be.

"When you're older."

I said, after a beat, a glance at the VCR clock, "I'm older."

He said, "When did that happen?"

"Right now."

He scooped me off the floor, held me to his chest, said, "But you're still just a baby, see?"

I laughed. He did too.

Placing me on the couch he told me that I needed to get ready, that it was almost time.

I knew what time it was, I'd checked. But I looked away from him, stared out the window at something, eyes wide, mouth hanging open. Mom would say I was catching flies. She eventually stopped saying that, though. But I liked hearing it. I laughed when Mom would said it. Dad did, too.

Staring outside I heard him saying something, knew he was talking to me. But there was something out that window.

"Buddy?" he said. He said it loud, nearly yelled it.

I flinched.

I asked him where my pin was, told him I needed to get ready.

He looked at me, eyebrow cocked, mouth flattened into a straight line. It was a new face. But I held out my hand pretending I didn't notice.

Dad handed me my communicator pin. A real one. Like they wore on the show. Metal and sharp. And shiny. Gripped between my thumb and pointer finger, I stared at it. When I tipped my pointer a bead of light skimmed the metal edge up to the tip of the pin. When I dipped my thumb the light slid back down.

He took the pin out of my hands, unclasped the metal needle. He smiled, pinned it to my shirt.

Tapping his own pin he said, "Captain to bridge," and looked to me.

"Two to beam up," I said.

Dad turned on the TV and sat next to me on the couch.

Captain Picard began speaking. The camera panned over millions, billions of stars. Then the *Enterprise* shot at us going warp speed. I jumped. And laughed.

I didn't see Mom come in the room. I didn't see her sit down. I don't remember her being next to me at all until she muted the TV.

"Milo," she said. "Did you hear me?"

I said no. I asked her why she did that.

She looked at my dad. And Dad looked at me.

I snatched the remote and turned the volume back up.

• • •

I tell Mr. Moore I'm nervous when I reach out and shake his hand.

He tells me there's no need at all to be nervous.

"Yeah, right," I say.

There are people behind me. I don't mean to hold any of them up, but this is too big. I feel stupid sweating through my uniform, seeing Mr. Moore wipe the sweat I left on his hand onto his pant leg.

"Nice uniform," Mr. Moore says. "Looks authentic."

I tell him it is. That I got it off Etsy. It was based off the actual templates used for the show. I say, "It's a little tight. I don't know how Edward James Olmos felt comfortable in it with that big belly of his."

Mr. Moore laughs, sips coffee from a Styrofoam cup.

If you look close enough, Styrofoam looks like millions of white plant cells magnified a thousand times. Even without a microscope the little cells are on display. They're uniformed and perfect, molded together to fit any shape. Cups. Molds for action figures. Packing peanuts.

Mr. Moore asks me if I'm okay.

"What? Oh, yes. Sorry."

"Anything else I can do for you?"

I stuffed nearly a dozen scripts in my bag before I left my dorm this morning, just in case somebody important happened to be here. It's been a while since I sent them out. I figured I wouldn't hear much back from anyone I sent it to. Sending scripts to random slush piles doesn't yield great results. I read that on the internet.

Pushing a copy of my script across the flakeboard table I tell Mr. Moore that I hope he is interested in this. I say, "I think you're perfect for it. After what you were able to do with *Battlestar Galactica*."

"*Lost in Space?*"

"I actually can't believe you're here. I didn't see you on the list."

"Late addition."

"I figured New York, maybe. But Philly? If it was New York we wouldn't be talking right now."

A guy behind me clears his throat.

Mr. Moore asks me what I want him to do with the script.

"I freaked out the *Firefly* cast up there last year," I say.

He asks me my name.

"Then I made a scene," I say.

Mr. Moore looks past me.

Someone taps me on the shoulder. I slap the hand away, take a breath, apologize to Mr. Moore.

He says it's okay. "But there is a line," he says.

"Yeah. Sorry. Just one more minute, though. Please."

I leaf through the script, hear people behind me complaining. Grumbling. But I keep going. I detail a scene in which Major West and Dr. Smith get into a brutal confrontation after the *Jupiter 2* gets lost. West blames Smith, threatens to put him out an airlock. He then beats Smith until he notices Will watching. The boy, terrified, can't take his eyes from Smith's bloody face. This will cement Will's and Smith's student/mentor relationship. Even though Smith will time after time betray Will's trust.

Behind Mr. Moore, just over his shoulder, a Jedi Knight and a Sith Lord begin to duel. Their lightsabers sputter tinny movie sound effects from speakers in the hilts. Superman comes between them, breaks them up. He begins speaking. But I can't hear him. I imagine he's reasoning with them, telling them that battling one another isn't the way to solve their issues.

Someone says hello. To me, I think.

When Superman walks away, the Jedi and Sith reignite their lightsabers, and their undying hatred.

"Hello?" Mr. Moore says.

"Sorry," I say.

"Normally," he says. "A pitch is only about two sentences long."

I say okay, say, "Family gets lost in space. They try to find their way home."

I feel a hand on my shoulder again, and I whip around out of my seat. Thor, blond wig in his face, tells me time's up.

I shove him, my hands hitting him in the center of his chest. He crashes into Mr. Spock, who stumbles back into Marty McFly. The rest of the line goes down after that, collapsing into a heap of primary colors and fake hair.

Mr. Moore, now standing, catches flies without blinking.

I tell him all my contact information is on the cover page.

• • •

When I was younger I kept a notebook next to my bed.

I spent the hours between going to bed and getting ready for school writing. Not being able to sleep I would concentrate on something like it was the only thing on Earth, then move on to the next thing, and the next thing. I remember writing a *Star Wars* novel. And a *Quantum Leap* script. A seventh *Star Trek* for the original cast.

I was in the middle of writing a *Lost in Space* story from Robot's perspective one night. In the story, Robot watched Will and Dr. Robinson working to build a time machine to get them back to Earth before they left in order to stop themselves from ever leaving. Nothing much happened. Robot just watched them working together, enjoying each other's company despite their situation.

I heard the toilet flush across the hall.

From my bedroom door, Dad in the bathroom standing over the toilet, staring into the bowl. He jumped, said, "Christ."

"Sorry."

He caught his breath, jammed an empty pill bottle into the pocket of his pajama bottoms.

I asked him if the pills he flushed were mine.

He said, "Can't sleep?"
I shook my head, looked at the floor.
"That happen a lot?" he said.
I nodded.
"A lot, a lot?"
"Almost all the time."

He knelt down, put his hands on my shoulders. He hadn't been shaving, his skin was pale. He asked me if I wanted to watch TV with him, said Sci-Fi runs *Lost in Space* in the middle of the night.

"Yeah," I said, staring into his face, at the bags under his eyes, the sweat on his forehead.

He shushed me, his finger pressed to his lips. "Don't tell Mom about this," he said shooing me down the stairs.

I asked him what I wasn't supposed to tell Mom about.

"Any of this," he said.

• • •

Dad says, "You punched Thor?"
"I pushed Thor."

The streetlights brighten the car as we pass under them. Dad stares straight ahead, driving, saying nothing.

The car lights up again.

I tell him to say something.

"I have nothing to say."

We're in the dark again.

Another streetlight, more light in the car.

I say, "I didn't mean to."

I tap a drum beat onto the center console. It's fast, manic, keeping me in the car.

Dad's driving faster; the light fills the car and dissipates faster, faster. He says something, but I don't hear him. There's only the light from the lamps we pass under, the darkness that fills the space when we're in between them.

Dad honks the horn once, twice, screaming my name. "Wake up," he says. "Listen to me when I'm talking to you."

"Sorry," I say.

"That's all you can say?"

"What else am I supposed to say?"

"We're putting you on medicine. Again."

"Why?"

He slams the butt of his palm into the steering wheel, curses. He pulls the car over, tells me I'm a mess. Says normal people don't stay in college this long, they don't need to. "All you talk about," he says, "is bullshit. None of it matters."

I don't say anything.

He says things like, "Antisocial."

Like, "Strange."

Like, "Selfish."

I flinch every time he spits a new word at me.

I say, "It's your fault."

When I open the car door at a red light he asks me what the hell I think I'm doing. I slam the door in his face, cutting him off.

Then I run.

I take off down the road, cut into the woods, and keep moving until my lungs don't pull any air, my legs turn to rubber.

In the woods, there's nothing to see in the dark. There's nothing to stare at. I'm alone, trying to concentrate on breathing.

Hands on my hips, teeth bared, sucking back air, I tip my head back. Up past the tops of the trees there's nothing but stars. And they rope me in. They make me lie down. Get lost.

My phone rings in my pocket. The theme from *Star Trek*.

I ignore it.

It begins again, but I barely notice it.

Eventually I don't notice anything at all.

• • •

"Will said, 'Dad, the time machine's done.' Dr. Robinson smiled at Will. He put his arm around Will's shoulder and said, 'Are you ready, son?'" I said this, reading from printed pages, holding them in my sweating hands. I was flicking the bottom corners of the pages with my fingers. John Williams' *Star Wars* in swishing paper.

Dad was sitting on the couch in front of me, clean shaven and put together. But eyes were lazy, half closed. His lips were pressed together. Like he was holding something in.

"Then," I said, reading from the page, "Robot watched as they stepped into the machine and went back in time together and stopped themselves from ever getting lost. The End."

Mom, leaning against the frame of the entrance into the dining room, clapped her hands. She said it was great.

"It's old," I said.

She said I should try and write a sequel.

I said, "But there's no more to the story. That's it. They fixed everything."

"There are always consequences when people disturb the time stream. Something goes wrong. Always."

"Nothing goes wrong."

Dad stands up, walks past me, says, "They did that in the movie."

"What?"

"The movie. It was all about trying to go back in time to fix things. You ripped off the movie. And it hasn't even come out on tape yet."

Mom said Dad's name.

Dad didn't even turn his head to look. He said, "Aren't you getting a little old for this stuff?"

I wanted to say no, ask him why he said that, tell him if I'm too old for it, so is he. But the grain running through the hardwood floor, all of it, pointed toward the kitchen. I checked. I scanned all of the planks. I could hear my parents' voices, someone knocking on a wall. But my eyes were following the rivers of wood grain from my feet, under my parents', toward the kitchen.

The floor loosened its grip on me, and I heard Dad say, "Forget it. He's gone."

• • •

I'm typing, ignoring the red and green lines appearing under my sentences. My leg bounces, knee bumping the bottom of my desk, each collision a metal ding.

There's something else. Knocking wood. Somewhere out there. Faraway.

Dad says my name from the other side of the door.

"I'm not here."

"Milo. Come on."

I lean back in my chair, reach for the doorknob and turn it, let the door hang open, let in the noise from the dorm.

He's inside now. I hear him. I don't turn around to see him staring at the duct tape X's on the floor where I don't like to stand. Or the cave I built with the extra desk in the room for when I hear just about everything happening all over the world all at once. Or the glow-in-the-dark stars I stuck to the ceiling after I made it out of the woods.

Dad says something came to the house for me, says, "I read it."

The open envelope he hands me has no return address.

Dear Milo,

I read your script despite what happened at the convention. It's good. You should be proud of it. But...

It keeps going from the there. I drop it in the trashcan next to my desk.

Behind me, Dad says, "Now why'd you go and do that?"

"Thought that's what you'd want me to do."

Dad tells me to turn around. And I do. But I don't look at him.

He says, "What are you working on there?"

Black bags under his eyes. Stubble darkening his face. A Best Buy bag is wrapped around his hand.

"A script," I say.

He asks me if it's another *Lost in Space*.

"Actually, yeah. It's an episode where Will and Dr. Robinson get separated from the..."

Dad tells me to keep going.

And I do.

And he listens.

Asks questions.

Above the sagging blackened skin, his eyes come alive. And he smiles with his teeth.

I get up, acting out the scenes that need visual aids. And Dad watches the entire time. He doesn't interrupt.

After I'm finished, once I sit down, he tells me it's good. "I really like it," he says.

I point to the bag in his hand, ask him what it is.

In the bag is a box with the Robinson family in their yellow and purple, green and pink uniforms smiling at me. Dr. Smith, in his black and purple, glares at the camera, arms crossed over his chest.

I turn the box over, read the back, turn it again and lock eyes with the family.

"Thought we could watch a few," Dad says.

I don't say anything. I barely hear him.

Dad wipes the sweat from his forehead, takes a breath, looks as if he's struggling to speak. He clears his throat. Using an older, raspier version of the voice I remember, Dad says, "Want to go home and watch a few with me?"

And despite my eyes moving from his shaking hands, his nervous eyes, the sweat, I hear every syllable.

Darwin

During his math test, Darwin talks about watching his favorite shows on Hoolahoo. The one about the lightning guy in red is his favorite. The guy who can run real fast, cross between dibensions, time trabble.

His repaired cleft lip slurs his speech, makes his Double-Yoos Wubbleyous. Ars, Awes. Makes other kids do impressions of him when there aren't any adults around.

Even with adults around, they whisper, giggle.

But Darwin doesn't mind.

He says he wishes he could run fast like the lightning guy. Says he'd play jokes on all the kids in class to make them laugh. He says, "Then I'd go back in time and do it again. The same joke over and over. So they could laugh forever."

He says he wishes he could zoom into the schoolyard to stop bullies. Flash into a room wearing all red, crackling with golden electricity to stop fights. Be something to somebody at precisely the moment they may need him.

But Darwin doesn't run fast.

He can't time travel.

Can't spring into action to right wrongs.

He's short. Slow. Clumsy. Pudgy.

But when they laugh, he smiles.

It doesn't matter to him why they're laughing either. Darwin will smile like he's living a dozen lifetimes in one moment. Over and over and over. Nothing but teeth and watery eyes and aching stomach muscles forever.

Death Protects

It was on the news.
No one was named.
Nothing was solved.
People were dead and it was back to Sheena Parveen for the weather report—it was going to feel like Christmas should've.

• • •

"Motherfucker from his block did it," Derrick said before first period. "Put three in him."
I almost said, "Derrick. Language." But didn't.
A bell. Chairs scraping against linoleum. Whispers of James' death before I got started.
I'd prepped a Powerpoint. Held a discussion about Lennie Small's brains getting blown out. Why George would do that. How death protects from pain.
Marcy excused herself without a pass.
I said nothing, sat down. Wiped a coffee ring off my desk, filed stray papers.

• • •

Over the PA, a senior assembly in place of fourth.
Principal Adler talked about James. Used words like Senseless, and Future, and Cope.
There were tears from students, other teachers.

People signed up for sessions with the grief counselors brought in for the day.

We'd pick back up with *Of Mice and Men* tomorrow.

• • •

The English department offices were filled with sniffling, stories, comments about James' papers—insightful for his age.

Matt said, "You had him, right?"

Sue said, "Good kid, wasn't he?"

Chris said, "What are you thinking?"

I answered the questions. Told the truth. All good things.

Then, in his office, I told Chris that once this sort of thing happens enough it's just cloudiness. Hypersensitive ears. Waiting for everyone to go back to normal.

• • •

The students were dismissed early.

We were asked to stay.

Figured I'd leave before I was allowed.

I smoked out back where the cameras had been ripped from the walls. Watched trash tumble down the filthy street. Homeless rummaging through mounds of garbage. People collecting on corners, handing things off, moving along. All concrete, brick, and cinder block. Chain link fences and caution tape.

Gray, cold, everything amplified by the squalor.

James got three put in him.

He was the third since September.

• • •

I had to Xerox a quiz.

I left anyway.

Walked over the glass in the parking lot. Kicked a syringe into a pile of dead leaves. Crushed a beer can as it rolled my way with the wind.

I'd go home. Work through my DVR. Drink coffee. Go to sleep with Nick at Nite casting a blue glow onto my bedroom walls in the dark. Then I'd wake up in the morning, go to work, and give a lecture on death and what it means and how sometimes it means nothing and how sometimes it loses meaning.

Alone in front of my car, my reflection in the window, I showed myself my teeth, arched the corners of my lips and turned my mouth into an inverted U, made a face people make when they cry—a face I never used to have to think about making.

Then I got in the car, started it up.

I drove home listening to the tires' white noise on the road.

Coffee Mug

    The inside of her mug's caked in stains every shade of brown. Think, a dig for ancient whatevers in a desert.
    She takes her first morning Columbian black.
    Her second with five(ish) sugar packets.
    Her third and fourth, a little cream.
    The t-shirt/flower-print scarf combo work-ensemble makes her almost fictional. Almost. Disheveled, jittery, she lifts her mug from her desk to her face, desk, to face. She talks Twenties, and flappers, and diaphragms. If this were a novel, nobody'd believe she were real.
    And all day her mug makes more new rings on her desk.
    Mug crust shows her yesterday, and last week, and last month through her afternoon green tea. Think, staring down through nearly clear water at the ocean floor somewhere not here.
    The sun catches dozens of interlaced rings of grit melting into a map of time by the end of the day.
    Past, present, no future.
    But tomorrow, more history.

He's Doing Just Fine

Nate's doing great.

He has strategies. He knows his triggers. He keeps a little red notebook in his back pocket. He picked that one up during his ninety-day stint.

His counselor said, "It's a good tool to maintain a level of self-awareness you may not have had in the past."

His support group leader said, "All adults struggle with the difference between knowing who they are, and what they think they can handle."

But it was also said that addiction doesn't take sick-days, and the notebook's a reminder.

So Nate scribbles notes, makes lists. There's a list of things he shouldn't do anymore. There's a list of place he can't go. There's quite a bit of overlap between the two.

He writes, Jason's house.

Then, Medusa Lounge.

Then, Jersey.

Nate's encouraged to show his notes to his family members. Just so they know that A.) He's doing what he's supposed to during this crucial post-rehab period, and B.) They can provide any assistance they need to if ever he makes the decision to return to his old habits.

His father says, "You used to love the beach."

His mother says, "You loved the boardwalk."

And Nate says he never wants to smell the stink of that state again. He says, "Plus Jason always got his stuff over there."

His father says, "Don't talk to Jason anymore."

His mother says, "Already on the list, see? Good for you, Nathan."

Nate's brother Tony calls, says he's not making dinner tonight, says he can't talk. So Nate, his mother and father, eat a pasta dish his mother always makes when there's something to celebrate. They talk about how nice it is to have Nate home again.

"How's Tony?" Nate says.

His father says, "You know Tony. He's standoffish."

His mother says, "Stop it. He's just busy. He works hard."

"That's new," his father says. He winks at Nate. "He's trying it out."

Nate's mother reaches across the table, slaps his father's hand, says, "Stop it. Try calling him up, Nathan."

Nate doesn't tell her he had called. A couple times. Left messages from rehab. He would text now, but the papers he signed explained he no longer has the privilege to own or use a cell phone. By the time he's able to use one again it may very well need to be implanted in his ear—or his eye. Unless, of course, the judge views the progress he's making as permanent change. Not the Band-Aiding of a wound that'll get ripped open every other every-so-often.

Nate eats, tells his mother the food's delicious, says he's going to go write a bit.

Before, any excuse to leave a room would mean something else. So his parents stare a moment before seeming to remember the progress he's making. They smile. They nod. And Nate steps out of the kitchen, passes photos on the foyer walls. In one he's featured in a football uniform. Another, he's holding an oar with the rest of his rowing team. A third, in a cap and gown, his arm is wrapped around his pimple-faced little brother's shoulder.

In the room he slept in as a kid, he writes another list.

Ways to Make Everything Up to Tony.

He writes, Save up, replace stuff I stole.

Then, Apologize. For everything.

Then, as an addendum, he writes, Don't fuck up.

• • •

Nate's making excellent progress.

His former boss says he's heard as much while they shake hands. "I want to do this," the boss says. "I don't have to."

Nate nods. His father, beside him, does the same.

"Your dad's a good man. I trust him."

Nate's father shakes his head, mouths, no, no, no.

"We're going to reinstate you."

"Thank you," Nate says.

"Under three conditions. One. You'll be under probation until your court date. Since we don't know what will happen, you'll be taken off probation only if you return."

Nate says, "Okay."

His father says, "That's fair."

"Two. Weekly and random drug tests."

Nate says he has to do that anyway.

"And three. If at any moment there is evidence of a relapse, no matter what the circumstance, you're out. Whether you're standing funny enough for people to think something's up, or you look just a bit too sleepy, that's it."

"I understand."

His boss says, "I'm taking a risk. But I think it's a good one to take."

"Thanks, I—"

"Remember how many people are sticking their necks out for you."

"I will."

"Good. Now, out. See you in the morning."

Nate watches his father shake hands with the boss. They use each other's first names, they smile, they pat each other's shoulders. Nate stays still, stares at his father's face smiling and saying thank you.

In his notebook, Nate writes, Learn to make/maintain positive relationships.

And, Stick out neck.

And, Take good risks.

His father asks him if he's ready to go.

The walk across the shop floor is filled with factory sounds that used to lull Nate to sleep. While he was standing. They pass people who filed complaints against Nate. They pass people who looked the other way on the real bad days. They pass a guy who said he'd quit if Nate ever walked into the building again.

Nate writes while he walks. When he's not writing, he's staring at the floor ahead of him. He'll make eye contact another time. Tomorrow. Or maybe only when he has to.

His father says, "You should be happy."

"I am."

"Then what's this about?"

Nate says nothing, sidesteps someone who says hello to his father, but not him.

His father says, "All you need to do is show them how much you've changed."

In the car, Nate sits on the passenger side. He writes that he can't remember what it's like being behind the wheel. He writes that he can't remember the last time he drove sober. How driving high felt. Every word is positive.

His father puts his hand on Nate's shoulder, says his name.

Nate's scratching notes into his notebook makes his father's voice sound as if he is speaking to him from inside a glass box. Filled with water.

His name is said a second time.

A third.

"Yeah?" Nate says. "Sorry."

His father doesn't say anything for a moment. Like he used to when Nate was high, after Nate would have to blink himself into understanding where he was and how he got there. Then his father says, "We need to talk about money."

Nate doesn't argue when he's told that his paychecks will be deposited into an account that he won't be able to access. That money will be taken from the account using a debit card his father will control. That Nate will be handed cash to buy lunch while at work. That he'll need to give up the change. That his earnings will be socked away for the future. It's unclear if that means until there is little doubt that Nate will relapse. Or that he'll have to be given an allowance by his parents for the rest of his life.

Nate nods his head, says, "Okay."

His father says, "I hope you're not looking at this as punishment."

"No. I did this to myself. I was just hoping—"

"What? Hoping to what?"

High, Nate would laugh whenever his father's voice went urgent. It's still a bit funny. But he doesn't laugh. He keeps his face straight by crossing off the list item regarding Tony's repayment. He writes, Figure something else out.

Nate says, "Nothing. I understand."

• • •

Nate is taking on responsibilities.

He tells his parents he's planning on going through all of the junk in the basement to find some things worth keeping. And others worthy of a trash bag.

His mother says, "Good for you, Nathan."

His father says, "You're crossing things off my honey-do list. Clean out all the junk-drawers around here for me when you're done."

In the basement, Nate digs through boxes of Transformers with pieces missing, preventing them from transforming to vehicle mode. He goes through a bin of Ghostbusters figures that stay or go depending on discoloration and nostalgia. He tosses Mighty Max playsets, motorized board games with battery acid caked on the pieces, Power Rangers with missing arms, or legs, or heads.

And he works every day after he and his father come home from the shop unless they work doubles.

He's told at his meetings that the formation of good habits will overrule the bad ones.

He's told that strides toward recovery—while they may seem small—are in fact creating a path that he can follow if ever he feels himself slipping.

But walking on ice is fucking hard.

When Tony stops by, Nate hears his parents upstairs telling his brother about all of that—everything they've read in his notebook, anyway. They use all the words he's heard over and over. All repetitive, but all positive. And he hears Tony say, "Good," and, "Glad to hear it," and, "I guess he's busy, I'll take off."

Nate listens to the muffled voices, works through a box full of Ninja Turtles. Figures, and vehicles, and pointy weapons that shouldn't have been included with kids' toys. Then, the costumes. Old foam turtle shells. Cloth masks with green plastic noses attached. Nate always wore red.

He ties the mask around his head, tries to ignore the mildew latching onto his nose hairs. Then he waits for the conversation upstairs—which at this point sounds like an argument—to end. But that could just be how the words seep through the floorboards.

The door opens. And Nate waits for the footsteps to end.

He jumps out from a closet, yells cowabunga dude, and scares the shit out of his brother.

"Holy shit," Tony says. "Fuck."

Tony's cursing is familiar. Nate heard it when he sold off most of Tony's CD collection. When he pulled out and pawned Tony's car stereo. When he emptied out Tony's checking account by assuming that he—like the rest of the family—used his birth year as the ATM pin.

"Sorry," Nate says. "Look what I found." He holds an orange mask out for Tony to take. "You can keep it if you want."

"That's a little small for you."

Nate takes off his mask, pulls it up over his head by the nose, says, "The shell's in here, too. You want it?"

"Thanks. But, no. I don't think I have anywhere to put it."

Nate swallows, shakes his head, looks at the floor. "Yeah," he says. "I'll probably just throw it out anyway."

Tony holds out his hand. Nate puts the orange mask in it.

"No, here," Tony says. They shake hands with their lefts.

Nate says, "How are you?"

"Good. You good?"

"Yeah. I'm good."

"Good."

"Yeah."

"Glad you're home."

"Me too."

"Sorry I haven't returned your calls. Things get crazy sometimes. You know."

"No. No problem. It's fine."

They talk a bit longer. About nothing. Pleasantries. Work. They don't get any closer than a handshake apart. And after a pause, Tony goes into how much he needs to do tonight.

Nate says, "Before you go. I wonder if there's anything I can—"

"Don't worry about it, okay?"

"You don't know what I was going to say."

"Yeah, I do. I know how those programs work. And it's fine. I'm fine. We're good. You don't need to make up for anything."

"It's not really the program that makes to me want to—"

"I'm not someone you need to worry about." Tony extends his hand again, says, "Let's get dinner sometime, okay? Just give me a call."

Nate shakes his hand, doesn't look into his eyes, says, "Yeah, I'll call you."

Once Tony is upstairs saying goodbye to their parents, Nate gets back to work. With a Sharpie he scratches Tony's name into the side of a box. He puts the orange Ninja Turtles mask, a foam shell, a pair of plastic nunchuks inside. Then he roots through the stuff he's already thrown into trash bags trying to remember which toys were his brother's.

• • •

Nate's doing just fine.

The calls to Tony that go unreturned don't stop him from going to group, seeing his counselor, going to work sober. Wishing he was high, but staying straight. They don't stop him from discussing realistic options with his lawyer.

And he does have options.

Plead guilty. Or don't.

His lawyer says, "It won't be as bad if you plead guilty."

Nate doesn't feel his face change. It's not as if he's surprised. But to his sides he can almost hear his parents' faces sliding off tensed muscle while the lawyer's words soak into their brains.

Nate's mother says, "What is he looking at, at best, if he does that?"

"Couple years. Parole."

Nate's father says, "There's nothing that can be done? Even with all the progress he's making?"

"Progress is great. Really," the lawyer says. But then he begins discussing the massive destruction of property. That not only was Nate high and driving, but he left the paraphernalia with which to get high in the car. "Yes, you went through a program. Yes, you've been conditionally released. But there is a reality here that we could fight and lose."

Nate stops his parents from speaking, says, "I still have time at home. I'm fine with this. I understand it, and I'm fine."

His father excuses himself to the bathroom, blames being an aging male.

His mother dabs her eyes with tissues from a pack she pulls from her purse.

And Nate shakes hands with his lawyer, says he'll see him in a few weeks.

The ride home is quiet. Nate writes in the backseat while his parents listen to news radio. He writes about Tony lying about wanting to get lunch. He writes about calling Jason, getting sent to prison early. Then he writes about what he said in the lawyer's office.

There's time. Plenty of it.

He writes that he can still fix things.

• • •

Nate's adjusting very well.

Having to ride in the passenger seat as his father drives the long way to work—to avoid the empty lot that used to be a house—is routine now. It's better that he can't see the lot anyhow. It would bring back how it felt having to be pulled from the wrecked car embedded in the front of the house. It would bring back the EMTs having to examine him with his one arm handcuffed to a stretcher. It would bring back the family standing in the street staring and crying as the shattered support beams gave out and buried Nate's car with the master bedroom.

When he's at work, he's quiet. He says hello to people who say so first, but otherwise he keeps his eyes on the shop floor. And the machines he works on. And the change handed to him when he pays for his lunch. And the look on his father's face when he hands over a smaller amount, making sure it goes unnoticed.

What he keeps, he adds to his total. Then updates a list he keeps in a second notebook that he doesn't share with his parents.

Only $146.82 more until he can buy a used Nintendo 64 for Tony.

Only $113.04 before he can buy the Nintendo 3DS that'll have to make up for the Game Boy Advance.

Only $27.69 before he can replace the VCR with a DVD player.

The list is long, but he's doing well with his priorities.

Then again his court date is coming up. And even though they go the long way home, there's the amount he'll have to pay in restitution. There's the amount of time he will spend in jail. There's the possibility that after a couple years in a cell, Tony will change his number to save himself from having to ignore Nate's calls.

At home, Nate watches his parents. How they act. How their vigilance slips with his progress. He's just doing so well with everything.

He has to remind his parents to check his notebook—the official one—a time or two.

His father leaves the car keys on the kitchen table for almost a half an hour, but curses about it later.

His mother lets him alone in the basement without calling down, asking how he's doing for longer stretches.

And Nate keeps track in that second book. Sitting alone in the unfinished basement, all cement and two-by-fours, Nate sits and scribbles. His red mask tied around his head.

He writes, Time's running out. I've wasted all my time.

Then it's the footsteps on the stairs.

Nate hides the notebook next to an envelope filled with the money he's saved behind boxes labeled Tony.

His father says, "Everything okay down here?"

"Hmm? Yeah, why?"

"What's with the mask?"

Nate pulls the mask off of his face, says, "Nothing. Just memories."

"Dinner's ready."

His father looks funny. Not the funny Nate remembers while coming down during holiday dinners. But funny.

He says, "Dad?"

"Yeah?"

"Do you think I could use some of my money to replace some of Tony's stuff? Like, the stuff I took."

His father smiles, walks across the room, puts his hands on Nate's shoulders. He did that when Nate was in high school. Less in college—not at all after he was kicked out. But, now, enough. And it's something Nate would miss if it disappeared again. His father says, "I think just being home and doing as well as you are is enough for your brother. Don't you?"

"I don't know if that's—"

"That's one area you don't have to worry about. Okay?

Nate lets out the breath he's holding, says, "Okay."

"Good."

The hand's taken away, his father's back is turned. Then his father says, "We're going to need that money for court fees, anyway. Know what I mean?"

Nate waits at the bottom of the steps, tells his parents he'll be right up. Then he drops his red mask into one of Tony's boxes.

· · ·

Nate is cultivating positive routines.

The day after of a week of doubles, Nate wakes up, tells his parents he'll be in the basement if they need him for anything. His mother asks him to stay upstairs, tells him he spends too much time down there anyway. "Why don't you watch TV with us this morning?"

"I told you I'd clean out the basement. I've been working too much, but I'm almost done." He closes the door behind him, ignores his mother's next sentence.

He stops at the bottom of the stairs. He checks the closets, the alcove with the water heater. The bare cement floors echo his footsteps more than he remembers. There's nothing for the sounds to bounce off but the floors and the walls. No trash bags filled with toys. No boxes marked with Tony's name. It's just Nate's voice calling for his parents that ping-pongs from wall to wall.

From the top of the stairs his mother tells him she thought she'd lend a hand, took everything to the dump during his double yesterday.

"What about Tony's stuff?" Nate says.

"I texted him about it," she says. "He didn't want any of it."

"Was there anything else? Did you find anything else?"

"That's why I wanted you to spend some time with us today."

Nate skips steps, pushes past his parents, yells at them, tells them that money was for Tony. No one else. "That was for him," he says.

He pulls the phone from the wall, dials Tony's number. It rings, and he screams things at his parents he hasn't since before his ninety days. He calls them, "You fucking people."

Tony's phone goes to voicemail.

Nate dials Tony again after dialing halfway through one of Jason's numbers.

"Nathan," his mother says, "Try to calm yourself."

"Calm your fucking self. I had a fucking plan. I was doing what I needed to do, and you fucked it up."

This Distance

His father says, "Don't talk to your mother like that." Hand on Nate's shoulder, he says, "We saw that second notebook, the money. We're just doing everything we can to make sure—"

Nate pushes his father away, points, says, "Shut. Up."

Over the phone, Nate begs Tony's voicemail to call him back. He says, "I need to talk to you," and, "Please stop ignoring me," and, "I'm your brother, man, come on."

Then he hangs up, leans against the wall, and slides to the floor.

Both his mother and father sit down next to him. Then it's all arms, and back rubs, and Nate screaming on the floor.

• • •

Nate's okay.

He goes to work, comes home, goes to bed, wakes up and does it over every day.

He hasn't added anything new to his notebook. He can't see a point to it anymore. Soon enough he'll be in a cell doing a multi-year sober stint. His track marks will fade all together. He'll put on weight. Maybe he'll get a degree.

He's reconnecting with old friends after his parents go to bed. Jason, who Nate wrote he would never be in touch with again, is nice, asks him how he's doing. And Nate says he's doing fine, but he needs a favor.

Since Nate stopped calling Tony, he's watched his father. Before work. During work. After work. Watching, taking mental notes. After double shifts, the guy's shot. He forgets things. He leaves stuff where he shouldn't. Car keys on end tables. Bills on the kitchen counters. Then his wallet in the master bathroom.

It's a matter of Nate telling his parents he's taking a shower after dinner. Then popping into the bathroom and replacing the orange PNC Bank card linked to his account with an old one from a junk drawer linked to nothing. Then standing under the water until enough time passes to suggest he did in fact shower.

He takes the trash to the end of the driveway. He leaves the card, wrapped in a sheet of paper telling Jason to try Nate's birth year as the pin.

Nate goes to bed nervous, but falls asleep over the possibility of feeling better. He wakes up early. Early enough to beat the sun outside. The mailbox holds the things he asked for, but the card wasn't left behind. He'll figure that one out later.

He waits until his father's alarm goes off to run into the bathroom. He jams his fingers down his throat, pukes up what little was left from dinner last night.

"You okay in there?" his father calls through the door.

"Yeah," Nate says, "But I think I caught something."

It's back to bed for Nate. His first sick day since being home. His father tells him not to worry about it, he'll explain everything. His mother tells him to reach her on the cell if he needs her.

Then he's alone.

Everything comes back to him. He's cooked up doses enough to ballpark his standard, functional high.

After, Nate will call Jason, ask what the fuck about the card.

After he can empty out his brain for a bit, he'll accept that he's heading to jail a little early.

After this, he'll call Tony, tell him not to worry about ignoring him, even though he's sure Tony's not worried about anything.

But for now he gets comfortable. He folds his legs, sits like he did in kindergarten. Then he's tying off an arm, slapping a vein swollen. Then he's poking through skin that's thickened up enough to send a signal to his brain telling him that shit hurts.

But the pain fades first. Then it's the room that blackens at the edges.

And he feels wonderful.

Nothing matters.

Nothing hurts.

And when Nate's chin meets his chest, everything sort of fades away.

The Slipper People

Sixth grade math and a bowl of Trix at the kitchen table.

The Trix were more important.

If it wasn't the cereal, it would have been something else. Cartoons. Nintendo. Anything. But none of that would've worked.

Mom needed everything looking better since the Slipper People had gotten worse. Dad needed everything calm at home, working until after midnight most days. And all my school assignments needed to be was done.

I wrote an answer on the homework sheet, didn't show my work, shoveled cereal into my mouth.

The milk changed color, the sweet-tasting chemical balls got bigger, the clock stayed still.

I got up, dumped more cereal in the bowl, sat in front of my homework, ate and pretended.

Everyone pretended then.

I could hear them upstairs. Stupid arguments. Nasty comments and laughter.

I didn't say hello when I'd gotten home.

Aunt Kath wouldn't have heard me anyway.

Gram would've said hello. Then said it again at dinner. During the Phillies game. Again before bed.

Upstairs, Kath told Gram she should shower, her voice loud enough for everyone in the neighborhood to hear but herself. A volume Mom would wince at during dinner on bad days. Volume Dad didn't ever have to hear.

Upstairs, Gram told Kath she was pain in the ass.

Kath laughed.

Minutes passed. Kath said, "Maggy, remember your shower."

Gram said, "I did that already."

"No. That was yesterday."

"Oh. Oh, shut up, Katherine."

They both laughed after that.

It'd used to be funny. When they'd first moved in. But after a school year, the silent dinners, the loud dinners, the Slipper People had stopped being funny.

It was the way they'd moved around the house, feet whispering over hardwood, carpet. Ghosts. It'd all become a pit in the gut. The feeling before puking, just bad enough to want to go bed and hope nothing happens.

Nothing was funny.

I still laughed though. Didn't need to know why.

So I sat, listened. Filled in homework answers using numbers from the problems so it looked like I was trying.

If Mom popped in, if I looked busy, if the Slipper People were quiet, tonight would be fine.

Kath turned on the shower upstairs, told Gram to get in.

English homework. Skimming the story, circling answers in a pattern, random enough to look real.

Upstairs Kath told Gram to make sure she takes off all of her clothes before getting under the water.

Gram said something, made Kath laugh. Laughing was all she could do. When she wasn't laughing she was staring. At the TV. At Gram. The floor.

She laughed a lot.

Like I did.

No written social studies homework; I didn't bother. But I opened the textbook. Stared at a page, waited a while, turned to another. Over and over until I got through the chapter.

If Mom hadn't started worrying the house was on fire, or one of the Slipper People had fallen down the steps, homework time would've been much more difficult. But she didn't need to be angrier—sadder—than she already was.

In science class, I'd learned that basic pattern recognition is one of the first things babies pick up. And I was in the junior high. I could do what had to be done. Had to.

Since the Depends in Mom's cart when we'd gone shopping for the Slipper People.

Since she'd started calling Dad, asking if he could quit the doubles.

Since she'd started asking me if I was doing okay during dinner, TV time, bedtime, while I was getting ready for school.

I got through my spelling words, my science definitions before Kath shuffled across the floorboards upstairs—all haunted house and scary movie sounds—and knocked on the bathroom door, opened it a crack, asked if everything was alright.

Gram yelled, told her she's almost done, called Kath a nuisance.

Then there was an argument.

I was out of my seat and stomping through the foyer. Standing at the bottom of the steps telling them to stop, telling them I was doing my homework. That I needed to concentrate. That Mom was going to cry again if they didn't cut it out.

I pounded my foot on the floor. Slapped my palm against the wall. Had to catch my breath.

Kath apologized. Added a Y to my name. Like she used to when I was a baby.

Gram said, "See that, Katharine? Always bothering somebody."

Kath said, "What?"

Gram said, "Close the door."

Kath said, "Huh?"

Then Gram asked what she was doing in the shower, said she'd showered already.

I walked away from the steps, my eyes stinging, my nose running, went back to the table to stare at my books.

Mom didn't pop in.

It was me and the phantom sounds over my head.

Then a drop of water smudging a sentence I wrote using one of my vocab words.

Another staining the yellow tablecloth mustard.

I moved my school stuff, tucked the paper into my folder in case Mom decided to check. But she didn't do that too much anymore. Just on good days.

Dad still checked. Made me do it over if it was sloppy.

But I didn't see him weekdays. A couple Saturdays a month. Most Sundays.

The drips from the ceiling turned to steady streams.

Bits of paint inflated. Matte-white balloons on the tips of hoses. They got bigger. Fatter.

The little water-sacks grew into a sagging bulge held up in center by the ceiling fan.

I didn't call Mom's office. She'd have lost it over the phone.

I went to the stairs. Said Kath's name. Turned back, couldn't say anything.

I moved into the living room, turned on the TV. Figured Mom would believe me if I told her I'd fallen asleep, didn't notice.

But I kept watching that blob. Slow, but growing.

I got up, went to the kitchen. Pulled a chair away from the table, stepped up onto it.

Sweating, temples pulsing, I poked that bubble thinking of waterbeds, bags of goldfish I'd won from carnivals when I was in kindergarten or first grade.

Then my finger went through.

At first it was water pouring out of the hole. Then the ceiling spit down the center of the hump, dumped water and white chunks all over the table. All over the kitchen floor. All over everything.

Kath didn't hear me calling her name, didn't hear me slamming the butt of my palm into the wall all the way up the steps.

Gram, her clothes stuck to her skin, said she wasn't even in the shower. And after I'd told her that's where she just was, and shut off shower spraying the soaked, warped bathroom floor hardwoods, she said, "I don't have to tell your mother you're fibbing, do I?"

I didn't call Mom.

I didn't clean up.

I sat on the couch and waited.

Through *Eek! The Cat* and *Extreme Ghostbusters* my knee bounced up and down, my face got blotchy, red, and wet. The water was still dripping from the ceiling onto everything. And Kath and Gram came down and asked what'd happened.

Once Mom got home, all the sounds were familiar. Her shoulder on the sticking door, her shoes on the floor. But she didn't say hello.

She stood in the kitchen, stared at the mess, at the hole in the ceiling. She said, "I forgot—I have to—I'll be back."

Then she left.

I was up, checking the windows for the car to drive down the street.

But it never did.

Kath said nothing.

Gram said hello, asked me when I'd gotten home.

At the side door, I held the curtains apart.

Mom was the in car. Her forehead was on the steering wheel. Her shoulders were shaking.

Then I was on the couch waiting for her to come back inside.

The TV off. Redoing my homework on the couch, crossing out my bad answers, trying to do them right.

I couldn't even do that.

But I'd promised myself I'd ask Mom to check it for me later. That I'd ask her to explain what I couldn't understand. That I'd show her I tried. Really, really tried.

I figured she'd like that.

Wake Up Dead

Taylor has a port, a pump, a box of syringes, and sore fingers. We—my husband Dan and I—we've got an app that can give us accurate blood sugar readings on a line graph as long as Taylor's iPod is connected to a Wi-Fi signal. And me, I've got a ceiling fan and my cell phone in the dark.

Stare long enough at a fan on high and the blades'll melt into a blurred circle, a single piece of wood running its circuit in slow motion. There but not there. Like a ghost. It's hypnotic, the effect. I'll stare and close my eyes and stare and close them longer. And by the time I'm drifting off, Dan already asleep, I'll sit up in the bed sweating, panting, checking my phone for any changes in Taylor's levels.

But of course, everything will be fine.

It always is.

And if it's not we'll fix it.

Tonight, like every night, we did every single thing we could before putting Taylor to bed. Gave him a snack—one that'll release sugars overnight to level out the dip he had and the shot we gave him. Waited until he was asleep-asleep before even thinking about getting underneath our own covers. Before I took my contacts out, even.

And when I wake up, Dan'll be so nice. He always is. He'll wake up and ask me what I need.

I'll tell him, no, nothing, everything's fine, that it's okay to go back to sleep. But I'll need to stare at that fan again to get back

This Distance

to sleep hoping Taylor won't pass without me knowing it. Hoping he won't phase through the bedroom wall all pale and see-through trying to tell me it wasn't my fault.

Taylor, my little ghost-boy, he'll be so sweet. He'll say, "Mommy, it was my bad pancreas. It wasn't you."

I'll sit up and cry, tell him that it couldn't have been. That I must've dosed him wrong before bedtime.

"No," he'll say. "Maybe the app didn't pick it up in time, but it definitely wasn't you, I promise. I just couldn't stay in my body anymore." He'll reach his hand out, white-blue and glowing in the muted television behind him. Like headlights through fog.

But my hand'll pass through his. All cold and clammy from the ectoplasm holding him together. And that'll just make it all that much worse. I'll never be able to touch him again. And it wouldn't matter how long he decides to haunt the house, he won't really be there. Not really.

No matter how many vases, or pizza boxes, or empty bottles he floats across the room just to get a reaction out of us.

No matter how much he spooks the dog into barking at the walls so he can giggle that giggle that makes me laugh.

No matter how many years in a row we win Best Haunted House in the Neighborhood Association Newsletter.

He'll have woken up dead.

Same for me. Every day.

A flesh and blood phantom talking to a specter of a little boy who died because of me.

"It was my blood," my little ghost-boy will say. "Not you. You did everything you could."

He'll tell me about how I left binders-full of log sheets for his daycare staff to fill out throughout the day.

He'll tell me about my mother, Gam-Gam, and how she whispers to herself that she can do it, she can do it, she can do it, when she gives him the shots I can't give him in the middle of the day.

He'll tell me about the day-long doctor appointments that I can't stand but smile through. The thousands and thousands of dollars spent on cutting-edge tech that insurance doesn't cover yet. The tears I don't let go of until Dan gets home and I'm in the tub with wine.

"I see everything now," Taylor will say. "I've seen everything you've done for me and I know, now that I'm dead, that none of this was ever your fault."

I'll change the subject, make a joke about his vocabulary, say, "It's impressive for a two-year-old."

"I'm infinite, Mommy," he'll say.

Then I'll cry harder.

Little boys aren't meant to be infinite. They're supposed to grow up, play sports, write poems for girls or boys they've fallen in love with. They're supposed to get in trouble, get caught smoking cigarettes, get questioned about the box of condoms stashed under their beds. They're supposed to go to college, pick absurd majors, work in bars to pay for their real degrees. Get married, get a dog, have a kid or two.

But Taylor, my sweet little ghost-boy, he'll be stuck like this. A blurry little body in the dark. Like the fan spinning overhead. An optical illusion. Real and not real at once.

And this time when I check my phone for any changes in Taylor's numbers, Dan doesn't wake up. I shouldn't expect him to. Not every time.

Sitting up soaked, the fan dries the sweaty ectoplasmic sheen off my skin. And when I catch a chill I check my phone again, the corners of the room.

No alert.

No ghost-boy.

Just me. Shivering, scared to go back to sleep.

I tip-toe across the floor, avoid the noisy spots. But they whine from under my feet no matter what I do.

The door creaks, but it's soft, low.

I catch my shadow in the hall, the w stretching my body twice my height, half my width. And when I reach for the doorknob into Taylor's room, my hand is a claw in the black.

But then it's the sound of little boy breath. Taylor dreaming in his crib.

My palm on his back, I feel his breath go in and out.
In and out.
In and out.
He's warm. Not sick warm. Alive warm.
The way he's supposed to be.
His soul still tethered to meat and blood and bone. No powers. No wisdom passed down through the infinite.
Just a boy.
Just like last night.
And the night before that.
I breath deep, close my eyes, let it go.
Like last night I say, "Stay here."
And like the night, before that I say, "Stay here."
And like I'll say it tomorrow night I say, "Stay here."

Acknowledgments

Thank you to Lizz, once again. She read early versions of these stories and, I'm sure, had to get particularly creative with her words of encouragement. But, as positivity is the color of her soul, whatever she said worked, and I kept working. That happens a lot. Like, a lot-a lot.

My mom and dad gave me the courage to follow a dream, to become a writer. I don't think they intended that I write stuff like this, though. Thank you, anyway. I'm not a sicko. Really. (Okay, maybe a little.)

Mallory Smart and Bulent Mourad. Guys, you've put up with me a second time. That must mean you like me! Well, I love you guys. Thank you.

Madeline Anthes edited all of these stories. Without her input, there would be no book. Joshua Isard, Katherine Hill, Nate Drenner, Andy Mark, Greg Oldfield, and Chad Towarnicki were integral to the completion of these stories as well. Thank you all.

Dean Steckel, you're next.

Zach Smith, I win. I'll have that meal now. Next year, I'm sure, I'll owe you.

Nothing's changed since *Good Grief* was released. You can still find me at Pizza Time Saloon in West Point, Pennsylvania, every Monday night, drinking beer with Michael Zakrzewski, Michael Mintzer, Jerred Snow, Josie Nagurney, Dave Bauer, Aaron Trieu, Dr. Joseph "J. Candy" Candelore, Todd Schatz,

David Boe, and Kyle Rodden. A guy like me couldn't ask for much more than friends like them. I look forward to Mondays. Who does that? I blame these scallywags.

Thank you to my entire, enormous family.

Nick Mehalick, Daniel DiFranco, Michael Mehalick. All I'm really trying to do is impress you guys.

Over the last four years I've had the pleasure of getting to know many, many folks in the literary community. Whether we've met in person, or only had to opportunity to communicate over the internet, their kindness, support, and encouragement has kept me inspired. Thank you to Francis Daulerio, Claire Hopple, Lynsey Morandin, Jeremy Bronaugh, Christopher DiCicco, Bud Smith, Tianna Grosch, Brent Rydin, Nick Farriella, Shan Cawley, Kailey Tedesco, Charlie Allison, Tracey Levine, Nick Perilli, Britny Brooks, Christina Rosso, Erica Peplin, Meghan Phillips, Justin Hunter, Jeremy Jusek, Zachary Woodard, and the dozens and dozens more I can't possibly list here without needing to fill several more pages. They're all putting terrific work into the world. Get out there and find some. Thank you to the following lit journals for publishing my stuff: Wyvern Lit, Pantheon Magazine, Driftwood Press, Crack the Spine, Yellow Chair Review, The Bitchin' Kitsch, Revolution John, Hypertrophic Literary, Donut Factory, Derail Literary Magazine, Rum Punch Press, Corvus Review, Dime Show Review, Third Point Press, Glass Kite Anthology, 805 Literary and Arts Journal, Random Sample Review, Ghost Parachute, After Happy Hour Review, Ellipsis Zine, and r.kv.r.y.

And, finally, thank you. You're great too.

—Nick Gregorio, 7/4/2018

Photo by Kyle Rodden

Nick Gregorio is a writer, teacher, reader, husband, hobbyist musician, and teeth-grinder living just outside of Philadelphia with his wife and dog. His fiction has appeared in many wonderful publications, and his first novel, Good Grief, was released by Maudlin House in 2017. He cohosts a podcast called book.record.beer, loves movies, punk rock, and comics, and buys more books than he has time to read. This Distance is his first collection of short stories.

For more, please visit www.nickgregorio.com

CPSIA information can be obtained
at www.ICGtesting.com
Printed in the USA
LVHW090536280821
696119LV00002B/77